NERD
CAMP
2.0

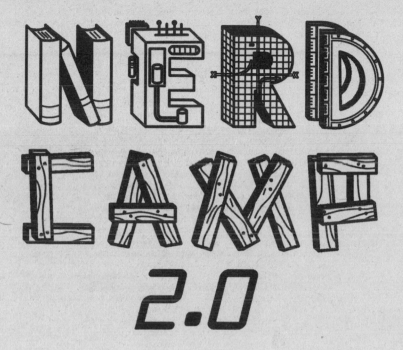

NERD CAMP 2.0

ELISSA BRENT WEISSMAN

Atheneum Books for Young Readers
New York London Toronto Sydney New Delhi

ATHENEUM BOOKS FOR YOUNG READERS
An imprint of Simon & Schuster Children's Publishing Division
1230 Avenue of the Americas, New York, New York 10020

For information about special discounts for bulk purchases, please contact Simon & Schuster Special Sales at 1-866-506-1949 or business@simonandschuster.com.
The Simon & Schuster Speakers Bureau can bring authors to your live event.
For more information or to book an event, contact the Simon & Schuster Speakers Bureau at 1-866-248-3049 or visit our website at www.simonspeakers.com.
Also available in an Atheneum Books for Young Readers hardcover edition.
Book design by Russell Gordon
The text for this book is set in ITC Cheltenham.
The illustrations for this book were rendered digitally.
Manufactured in the United States of America
0415 OFF
First Atheneum Books for Young Readers paperback edition May 2015
2 4 6 8 10 9 7 5 3 1
The Library of Congress has cataloged the hardcover edition as follows:
Weissman, Elissa Brent.
Nerd camp 2.0 / Elissa Brent Weissman. — First edition.
pages cm
Sequel to: Nerd camp.
Summary: Gabe has looked forward to another six glorious weeks at the Summer Center for Gifted Enrichment, but when a wildfire closes the nearby camp that Zack, Gabe's stepbrother, was supposed to attend, the Nerd Camp faces a "cool-kid invasion" that could mean big trouble.
ISBN 978-1-4424-5294-7 (hc)
ISBN 978-1-4424-5295-4 (pbk)
ISBN 978-1-4424-5296-1 (eBook)
[1. Camps—Fiction. 2. Ability—Fiction. 3. Stepbrothers—Fiction. 4. Interpersonal relations—Fiction. 5. Individuality—Fiction.] I. Title.
PZ7.W448182Net 2015
[Fic]—dc23
2014023025

For Lev

Chapter 1

ZACK

The main difference between Zack and his stepbrother, Gabe, could be summed up by baseball cards: Zack collected baseball cards to trade with his friends, while Gabe slid baseball cards under the strap of his night brace to prevent the headgear from itching his skull.

When Zack first saw that Gabe had brought baseball cards with him for his weekend in New York City, he was surprised and impressed. The stepbrothers finally had something in common. "You collect?" Zack asked. "Want to trade?"

"That'd be good," said Gabe. "Mine are starting to get permanent indents, and that defeats the purpose."

"What do you mean?" Zack asked.

Gabe took his night brace out of his duffel bag and wrapped it around his head, hooking it to pieces of metal on either side of his teeth. He then slid five baseball cards underneath the strap, from one ear to the other. "See?" he said. "I need to wear this whenever I'm at home, and all night. The fabric itches, though, so I put the cards underneath. An added bonus is that the cards keep my hair from getting too creased."

"Dude," said Zack. "With that thing on, I don't think anybody's looking at your hair."

"Ha-ha," said Gabe, removing the cards but not the headgear. "What do you do with your baseball cards, then?"

"I collect them," Zack said. "See?" He took out a small binder that was filled with pages of plastic sleeves. In each sleeve was a baseball card, and not one was creased or dented in any way. "My best ones are up front here, and they get worse as you go back. But sometimes I mix it up. I put some good ones toward the back so people won't know if I'm trying to give them my worst cards."

"What makes a card good or bad?" Gabe asked.

"Lots of things, like how good the player is, or if the card is rare. Some rare ones can be worth a ton of money, especially if they're old."

Gabe squinted through his bifocals and turned a couple of pages of the binder. "These look pretty new."

"Yeah, nobody can really afford old ones, since they're so expensive. Except for Leighton Ayres, who won't even trade with anyone because none of our cards are good enough for him." Zack rolled his eyes. "But my friend Nick found all these boxes of old cards in his basement, and his dad sold them for hundreds of bucks. That's what got everyone at school into collecting. And all those old cards were once new."

"Everything old was once new," Gabe said with wonder. "I'm taking a research methods class at camp this summer, and the first step of the scientific method is to make observations. That's a really good observation. Think about it. Really old books were once new books in stores. My mom's old camera that takes pictures on actual film, that was new once, and people probably thought it was really cool and the best way to take pictures. And artifacts! Think about those old pots at the Museum of Natural History. They were once new pots that people used for cooking."

Zack didn't understand why Gabe always had to think

about things so deeply. All he meant was that if he collected baseball cards now, eventually his new cards would be old cards that were worth money. But Gabe had to go off and talk about nerdy things like books and film cameras and pots at the ancient history museum.

When his mom first married Gabe's dad, Zack found it weird when Gabe did stuff like that, which was most of the time. It was bad enough that Zack had to move all the way across the country, leaving his friends and his dad in California to live in New York City. Their apartment was even smaller than it had been in LA, it took an hour and two trains to get to the beach, and his new school had kids who'd been in class together since kindergarten. If he had to get a stepbrother and make his family even more complicated, that stepbrother could at least be a built-in friend.

Looking back, it seemed stupid, but Zack had given a lot of thought to impressing his new stepbrother. He'd perfected his skateboard moves, set new high scores on his video games, and combed through his iPod, imagining himself going through Gabe's and finding all the same songs. Then he met Gabe. Gabe, who couldn't balance on a skateboard, who preferred books to video games, and who hadn't heard of a single band Zack liked. Nothing would have made the move easy, but was it too much to ask that Gabe be *a little* like him?

Now that they'd been stepbrothers for almost a whole year, Zack still thought Gabe liked nerdy things, but he was more used to it. That was just Gabe. He was on a math team (which Zack still didn't get, since math wasn't a sport) and went to a special summer camp that was like school, only with even more learning. But he was also fun and funny, and his nerdiness could be useful, like if you needed help with your homework or if you ran into a snake in the woods and needed to know if it was poisonous or not, which had really happened last summer. People made fun of nerds at school, but Zack liked hanging out with Gabe despite the geeky things he said and did. There was even something admirable about the way Gabe didn't try to hide that he was a nerd—not that he could hide it if he tried. Here he was doing something normal like looking at baseball cards, yet he was wearing headgear and talking about artifacts.

"Dude," said Zack. "Take off that night brace."

"Oh! I didn't even realize I was still wearing it. Good observation!" said Gabe. The metal on his teeth reflected into Zack's eyes as he unhooked the headgear from his braces and placed it on Zack's TV, which served as Gabe's nightstand when he visited. "It's actually not that uncomfortable, apart from the itchy strap. Last week my mom let me ride my bike up to the Italian ices place at night to meet Eric and Ashley, and I did the same thing. I passed these kids from school on the way and they laughed at me, but I didn't realize why until I got there and Ashley told me I was wearing it. It was pretty embarrassing."

"Did you have the baseball cards around the back too?" Zack asked.

"Yeah," Gabe said. Then he brightened. "At least my hair wasn't creased!"

Zack shook his head in disbelief. If that had happened to him, he'd beg his mom to let him move back to California. He made a silent promise to himself that when he got braces—which his mom said was going to happen in the fall, despite all his protesting—he'd put up with the braces and that's it. If the orthodontist tried to make him wear headgear or put on rubber bands or crank his teeth with a metal key every day, he'd flat out refuse. If that didn't work, he'd keeping "losing" his orthodontic equipment until his mom and the doctor got the picture.

Gabe sat down on the edge of Zack's bed. "What's the status of Mission: Campossible?" he asked.

"It's good!" said Zack. He was so pleased with Gabe's help in trying to get him permission to go to sleepaway camp that summer, he didn't even mind that Gabe had given their plan such a cheesy name. Without Gabe's help, all Zack would have done was beg and tell his mom that everyone else was allowed to go to camp, and he didn't think that would have swayed her to let him go. No begging would have changed the fact that he was still only eleven, and for some reason his mom had it in her head that he couldn't go until he was twelve. Gabe, however, was full of ideas, and he knew how to do fancy research that impressed adults. "I think all the stuff we've been doing is working," Zack said.

"Tell me!" Gabe said.

"Well," Zack said, "she really liked that list you helped me make, about how camp makes you a maturer person."

"The Camp-Builds-Character Proof," Gabe said proudly.

"Right," said Zack. "And last night I told her about all the camps we found that are right near yours, and I said how that'd make it easy to drop us off and pick us up together."

"Did the map help?" Gabe asked. He'd plotted the

locations of five camps near his own on a map to show just how close they were.

"Yeah, the map totally helped," Zack said. "Thanks, man."

"No biggie," said Gabe. "I've been working on one more thing, and I think it'll be the clincher." He made a drumroll noise on his duffel bag, then removed and unfolded a poster-size chart filled with numbers.

"Whoa," said Zack. "What's that?"

"Remember I asked you about all the stuff you'd do this summer if you didn't go to camp? Well, I added up the esti-mated cost of all those things, and then I compared the total to the average cost of going to sleepaway camp. I think the numbers speak for themselves."

Zack sat on the bed next to Gabe. He never knew why people said numbers spoke for themselves; he usually needed a teacher to speak for them. And even then he had a hard time listening, since there was so much other, more interesting stuff he could be thinking about, like what time it was in California, or how to perfect his boardslide at the skate park, or what color the hardened gum on the bottom of his desk might be. So he couldn't completely understand how Gabe's chart worked, but he saw lists of things that, he had to admit, would make an awesome summer: extra guitar lessons, a new skateboard, going to the beach and renting a surfboard every weekend, buying new video games, flying to LA to visit his dad. "This shows how much all this stuff would cost?" he asked.

"Yep," said Gabe. "I didn't know you collected baseball cards. I should add that to the list. But even without it, all the stuff you'd do at home adds up to a lot more than six weeks at sleepaway camp. I think your mom and my dad will see that the cost-effective approach is to let you go to camp."

"You mean it's cheaper to send me to camp than make me stay home?"

Gabe nodded. "Good observation."

Zack pulled the chart closer to him and punched Gabe in the arm. "Dude!" he said. "My mom is going to flip. Here's an observation: You're the best!"

"Thank you." Gabe said, beaming. He rubbed his arm. "And ouch."

Chapter 2
GABE

After his weekend with Zack, Gabe did the first thing he always did when he got back home: He gave his mom a big hug. He used to do it when he met his mom at Penn Station, but just as he was starting to feeling embarrassed about hugging his mom in the middle of New York City—where kids younger than him rode the subway without any parents—Gabe's mom decided that he was old enough to take the train from Penn Station back to Long Island by himself. He now first saw her in the car, and it was hard to hug someone who was sitting in the driver's seat, so he saved his big hug for right after they walked in the door of their house, but before he put down his duffel bag.

He was glad to be able to hug her in private, but he was also just glad to hug her. Even though it had only been one weekend, he always missed his mom while he was away. He loved spending time with his dad, and he liked his stepmom, Carla, just fine, but things were *different* there. The rules weren't as strict, for one thing. Gabe could drink as much soda as he wanted all day, not just one small glass when eating dinner at a restaurant. And he and Zack had a TV in their room, with cable and everything, which they could watch late at night or use to play video games. Gabe couldn't figure out why—and he'd spent a lot of time on the train trying—but for some reason it was easier to be at home, where he wasn't allowed to do as much.

"I missed you, Gabe," his mom said as they finished their hug. "What am I going to do when you're at Summer Center for six weeks?"

"I don't know," Gabe said. He dropped his duffel bag onto the floor and sat down on the couch. "But you have only fifty-eight days to figure it out."

"You leave for camp in fifty-eight days? I didn't know you were counting down."

"Fifty-eight days. Wesley's keeping track of hours and

Nikhil's counting minutes, so if you want to know more specifically, I can call them."

"That's okay," his mom said. "I don't think I could handle knowing how many hours. Though while you're gone, I may have to count the minutes until you get back." She gave him a kiss.

"Mom," Gabe said with a groan.

"You're right," she said. "Let's end this love fest so you can go unpack. Dirty clothes straight in the hamper, please."

Gabe e-mailed Wesley and Nikhil for the latest hour and minute update anyway. Thinking about camp made him wish he was there right now. His camp, the Summer Center for Gifted Enrichment, was like heaven. It was kind of like being at the gifted program at school, only without any non-GT kids walking by the door with their fingers in an L for "losers." And camp was every day and all day, from the morning wake-up siren until lights-out—or even overnight, since last summer his bunkmate Wesley solved math problems out loud in his sleep! This summer Gabe would be taking classes called "Research Methods" and "Heroes of Our World and Imaginations," which were sure to be stimulating. But the absolute best part—and there were lots and lots of next-best parts—was that everyone there was like Gabe. Last summer he'd spent a lot of time analyzing his camp adventures to determine whether or not Zack would find them nerdy. This summer he was determined to just relax and enjoy being surrounded by unashamedly geeky geeks.

Gabe thought more about Zack as he sorted his clothes into the white, light, and dark bins. He'd wanted a sibling forever, and having Zack didn't disappoint. Zack was super cool but also nice, and they always laughed a lot and did fun things together. Gabe wasn't as nervous about looking like a nerd now as he had been when he first met Zack; the first time they met he had to watch his every word, and all last summer he went to extremes to make sure Zack thought he was at a regular sleepaway camp, not what Zack would call "nerd camp."

Back then, Gabe thought as he dropped a pair of jeans in the pile of darks, it was like Zack was a white T-shirt and Gabe was a pair of dark jeans. Zack wouldn't dare mix with someone like Gabe. But now it was more like Zack was still the cool, crisp white shirt, but Gabe was the light blue shirt he was putting in the middle pile. He didn't have to hide the truth, but he was still constantly aware that he wasn't on Zack's level, so he tried not to act *too* nerdy during their weekends together. He'd brought his night brace and baseball cards, for instance, but he only put them on right before shutting off the light, instead of wearing them whenever he was home, like the orthodontist instructed. And when Zack talked about using his baseball cards for trading, Gabe didn't mention that a lot of his friends were into trading Element Cards; he knew Zack would find it geeky to try to collect cards to fill the entire periodic table. He noticed that Zack never invited other friends to hang out with them in Manhattan, but then again, the one time Zack came to visit Gabe on Long Island, Gabe didn't invite friends from school over either.

Summer Center, on the other hand, was like the whole pile of darks. There were kids who were as different as dark jeans and red shirts and striped pajamas, but they were all in a happy pile together. They all loved learning, and the coolest kids were the ones who loved learning the most. During class, they could speed through lessons because everyone caught on quickly, and the questions kids asked made the discussions deeper, not repetitive. During free time, campers memorized digits of pi and cracked jokes about history and turned a head lice epidemic into a science project. They'd probably all bring Element Cards this summer. Nobody worried about being a nerd, because Summer Center was nerd paradise.

According to the e-mails he'd gotten from Wesley and Nikhil, they'd all be there in fifty-eight days, twelve hours, and forty-two minutes. It couldn't come soon enough.

Chapter 3

ZACK

Zack called Gabe the minute he got the news. He often wished Gabe had a cell phone so he could text him instead, but this news was so exciting that he would have called no matter what.

"Dude!" said Zack. "We did it!"

Gabe gasped. "We did?"

"We totally did it! I was just sitting here, eating Chinese food, and my mom goes, 'So, Zack, do you still want to go to sleepaway camp this summer?' I literally dropped the piece of General Tso's chicken I was about to eat and said 'Yeah.' And my mom goes, 'Well, Chad and I have been thinking more about it, and I talked to your dad, and we decided that if you want to go, we think you're old enough to go.'"

"No way!" said Gabe.

"Way."

"Yes!" Gabe said. "That is so cool! What do you think did it? Was it the cost-comparison chart? I bet it was the cost-comparison chart."

"That was a big one. All of it helped! My mom said they think I should go to Camp Seneca because it's really close to your camp, and they start on the same weekend, so they can drive us both there together."

"They must have used the map!" Gabe said. "I didn't even think to look at start dates. I could have put them on the map too, using symbols and a legend of some sort. . . ."

"Don't worry, dude. We did it. I'm going!"

"You're going! We're both going to camp! And we'll drive there together, and we'll write letters back and forth, and maybe since the camps are so close, we can even visit each other one day."

"Yeah, that'd be awesome," Zack said. He glanced at the table. "Okay, I've got to go. We're still eating dinner, and I didn't even say thank you yet. And—shoot. Your dad is taking all the boneless spareribs. I'll talk to you later."

The thought of Gabe's camp gave Zack a pang of worry as he walked back to the kitchen. Camp Seneca was close to Gabe's camp—what if it was a nerd camp too? His mom didn't say anything about him taking a test to get in, but maybe this was a nerd camp for kids who weren't geniuses. Maybe it was like a summer-school camp, with lots of tutoring to try to make campers smarter. The thought of it made the boneless spareribs he managed to get from Chad lose their flavor.

Zack went to the Camp Seneca website right after dinner, and he was immediately put at ease. Camp Seneca had indoor and outdoor basketball courts, an archery range, a giant rock wall, a music studio with real recording equipment, and even a skate park! The list of activities was so long, he had to scroll down a few times to read them all, but apart from having a computer lab and library, not one of them sounded like something you'd have to do at school. The campers in the photos looked super cool, he could just tell.

This summer was going to be awesome.

Chapter 4

GABE

Eighteen days, twenty hours, fifty-six minutes, and twelve seconds (eleven seconds . . . ten seconds . . .) before Gabe was scheduled to leave for SCGE, a series of wildfires swept through the area of Upstate New York where the camp was located. Gabe heard about it while sitting at the kitchen table, doing some logic puzzles. His mom was preparing dinner, and the news was on TV in the background. They turned up the volume.

"In just a few weeks," the reporter said in front of a smoky backdrop, "thousands of children of all ages are set to descend upon the region to attend summer camp. The fire continues to blaze, and the extent of the damage will not be known until the firefighters get it under control. It remains to be seen whether the camps will be open—and safe—for the children's arrival."

Gabe stared at the screen, his mouth full of metal hanging open. "Fire?" he said.

His mom lowered the volume on the TV. "That looks like a terrible fire."

"I might not be able to go to camp?" Gabe asked. The thought made his lower lip quiver.

"We'll have to see," his mom said. "You can't go if there's a fire blazing in the woods."

"But," Gabe said. "But. But." He didn't know what to say. He had to go to camp. He'd been looking forward to it for 323 days. And what about Zack? His camp was in the same area, and he and Gabe had worked so hard to get him permission to go. "How will we know if we can go or not?" he asked

"I'm sure Summer Center will give us updates," his mom said. "Can you check your e-mail? Maybe they sent something."

"I'll check it after dinner. I doubt they have any news yet."

Gabe tried to concentrate on his logic puzzle, but now all he could think about was whether or not camp would happen, and what he would do if it didn't. He couldn't even remember what he did the nine whole summers he spent at home before he went to Summer Center. Obviously nothing memorable.

When Gabe's mom checked her e-mail after dinner, she reported that Summer Center sent a message to parents alerting them to the fires and saying they'd provide more information soon. Shortly after, Wesley sent an e-mail to Gabe and Nikhil saying, **Hey, Smarty, Geek, and Egghead—Let's figure out a way to fight the fire!!! I am going to diiiieee without SCGE!**

Nikhil replied, **I want to go too, but there's a FIRE there. They can't open the camp unless they are 100% positive the fire's gone and all the damage is fixed, just to be safe, right?**

Oh no, Gabe thought. Nikhil wouldn't do anything unless he was sure it was totally, absolutely, perfectly safe. Even if camp opened, Nikhil might decide it was too dangerous to go, and then things wouldn't be the same. **I'm SURE they won't open it unless it's 100% safe,** Gabe wrote back. **I just hope they open it!**

Their e-mails went back and forth like this all week, while the fires continued to blaze. Gabe also e-mailed with Zack, whose camp was in the danger zone too. Each message said pretty much the same thing: **I hope we get to go.**

On Friday, the director of Summer Center notified parents that the fires were under control, but they were assessing the damage to see if they'd be able to have camp. Gabe's arteries and ventricles pulsed with hope. There were still fifteen days until camp was supposed to start; with all the smart people working at Summer Center, surely they could assess the damage and get everything repaired in that amount of time.

Waiting for official news was hard, but at least Gabe still had school to keep him busy. He and his bunkmates continued their countdown, though Gabe could sense Nikhil's nervousness in his e-mails. One, sent very late at night, said, **You think they'll spend a few of the (roughly) 20,000 minutes before camp starts checking to make sure the lingering fumes aren't toxic, right? I signed up for the summer book club at my library, just in case they are toxic and theirs no Summer Center.**

Nikhil's next e-mail, sent less than a minute later, corrected the mistake in the last sentence. **In case THERE'S no Summer Center. The thought of toxic fumes is making me mix up basic homophones!**

Then, the following Wednesday morning, with only four

days left of school and T-minus ten days until camp, Gabe's mom yelled up to him from the computer. "Gabe!" she said. "Great news!"

Gabe froze with his toothbrush in the lower right quadrant of his mouth. He ran downstairs without bothering to spit out his toothpaste. "What is it?" he asked, his mouth full of froth.

"'We are happy to report,'" his mother read from the screen, "'that the Summer Center for Gifted Enrichment will go on as scheduled.'"

There was more, but Gabe didn't need to hear it. He shouted a loud "Wahoooo!" not caring that he was spraying toothpaste all over his shirt. He sang and did the cha-cha on his way back to the bathroom. "Ca-a-amp is o-on! Ca-a-amp is o-on!" Now he didn't even mind that school was ending—in fact, he could actually understand those people who couldn't wait for it to end! He once again had camp to look forward to.

Not even an e-mail from Amanda Wisznewski, the girl who'd followed him around last summer like a puffy-haired shadow, could ruin his mood. **Looks like we'll be at camp together again after all,** she wrote. **We really are meant to be.**

Chapter 5

ZACK

Zack checked the Camp Seneca website every day after school and again before going to bed, even after he heard from Gabe that Summer Center was going to happen. It always said the same, unhelpful thing: *We are assessing the damage from the wildfires and will be in touch with more information shortly.*

It wasn't fair. He and Gabe worked so hard to convince his mom to let him go to camp, and then he got really excited about it, and now it looked like he wouldn't get to go after all. If Camp Seneca was canceled, his summer was sure to be the most boring summer in the history of man. All his friends from school were going to sleepaway camp or traveling to fancy places with their families, and even the kids he still talked to from LA were doing cool things that didn't involve visiting him. Since he was supposed to go to camp, his mom didn't sign him up for any fun things to do in New York City, and now there were no spots left. Even the weeklong "summer experience" at his school, West Side Prep, was completely full. Not that he wanted to do that, anyway. All he wanted to do was go to Camp Seneca.

Zack could actually understand the kids like Gabe who wished school wouldn't end. At least school gave him something to do and friends to do it with, especially now that the big tests were over and they spent most of the day watching movies, cleaning out their desks, and trading baseball cards.

After his last day of school, Zack checked the Camp Seneca website again. *We are assessing the damage from the wildfires and will be in touch with more information shortly.*

Blargh. Gabe had heard from his camp almost a whole week ago. It figured that those smart people were able to "assess the damage" quicker, but really, a whole week?

"Any news?" his mom asked.

"No," Zack said, throwing himself back into the couch. Then he lifted his eyes in hope. "Can I go to a different sleep-away camp if Camp Seneca is closed?"

"I don't know, Zack. It's probably a little late to sign up, since they all start next week. Let's wait and hear from Camp Seneca."

"What if they don't tell us for another week and it's canceled? Then it'll *really* be too late to sign up for somewhere else."

"You said Gabe's camp is open, right? That probably means yours will be too."

"Whatever." Zack pushed the laptop away and turned on the TV. Like he needed a reminder that his stepbrother would be going to sleepaway camp and he wouldn't, *again*.

"I understand you're upset," his mom said, "but I hope you don't expect to just watch TV all summer."

"Mom," Zack said, "leave me alone."

"You've made so many nice friends here. I'm sure you'll have fun this summer even if you can't go to Camp Seneca."

"I don't want to talk about it." Zack turned off the TV, dropped the remote, and went into his room. Not going to sleepaway camp would mean spending the entire summer with his mom. It had been a whole year and she still hadn't gotten a job here in New York, so her only job was hanging around and trying to do things with Zack. He turned on the TV in his room by pressing the button so hard, it hurt his finger. Then he threw the remote across the room, causing the back to open and the batteries to roll under his bed. The whole situation was made even worse when he saw what was on: golf. It was like the universe was giving him a taste of how boring his summer would be.

Zack dropped to his stomach and reached for the batteries, but after coming back with a fist-size ball of dust, he gave up and lay on the floor, closing his eyes. The low, patient voices of the golf announcers on TV were kind of soothing. After a few minutes of nothing but breathing and golf, he was calm enough to remember that back when he thought he was going to camp (only two weeks ago, even though it seemed like ages), he knew he'd miss his mom while he was there. It wasn't her fault there were wildfires in Upstate New York, or that the camp still hadn't reported whether or not they'd be open. He knew he should apologize to her, but instead he just lay there and tried to forget about the whole thing.

He didn't leave his room until dinnertime, and he could tell his mom was still annoyed about his attitude from the way she served only herself lasagna and then sat down.

Zack cut himself a big square of lasagna and sat down next to her at the small table. "This looks really good, Mom," he said.

"Thank you."

He took a bite and made sure to swallow it before saying more. "I'm sorry I got mad at you before," he said. "I was just really looking forward to camp."

"I know, sweetie," she said, eating a bite herself and then smiling. "Which is why you should go look at the computer."

Zack's hand stopped on its way to his mouth. "What? Is there news?"

"There's news."

"As of when? Why didn't you tell me?"

His mom shrugged and kept eating, as though trying to suppress a smile.

Zack pushed his chair back, stopping himself midpush to ask if he could be excused, and then raced to the laptop. His mom's e-mail was open, and a message from "The Camp Seneca Team" filled the screen. Zack read as quickly as his eyes would let him.

Dear parents,

Thank you for your patience while we assessed the damage from the wildfires that ravaged our region. We write today with some good news and some bad news. We'll get the bad news out of the way first.

Camp Seneca was hit hard by the fires. Most of our sleeping cabins were partially destroyed, and a few were completely wiped out. Our dining hall and kitchen are in bad shape, and many of our popular activities, including the skate park and music-recording studio, need major repairs. The extent of the damage is too vast to have the campground ready for children this summer.

Zack stared at the screen, fighting back tears. *Why was my mom smiling about this?* he thought. *Maybe she never really wanted me to go.* Then he remembered that the start of the e-mail said there was some good news. He didn't know what good news could possibly follow that introduction, but he scrolled down and crossed his fingers.

Now for the good news. We couldn't stand the thought of not holding camp this summer, so we have been investigating other options. After talking with other camps in the area, we discovered that some of them were not nearly as hurt by the fire. One of them, the Summer Center for Gifted Enrichment (SCGE), has graciously offered to share their campground with us. We are still working out the exact details—for example, they have extra cabins for us, but depending on the number of Camp Seneca campers who choose to attend, we may also have makeshift bunks in other buildings. SCGE does not have all the same attractions as Camp Seneca (no skate park, for instance), but it still offers an array of state-of-the-art facilities that we are sure will make for a great summer for Seneca campers.

While we cannot say enough how grateful we are for SCGE to open its campground to the Camp Seneca community, we also assure you that your children will still be attending Camp Seneca, not SCGE. The two camps will remain independent in terms of daily activities and administration. Your children will have the full Camp Seneca experience, just in a different environment.

Zack skimmed the rest of the letter, which talked about price changes and discounts and deadlines, before rereading the part about sharing the SCGE campgrounds. He read it three times, but he still wasn't sure if it was good news or bad.

Back at the table, his mom was finishing up her lasagna and starting on a salad. She liked to eat dinner backward, which was fine with Zack. Most nights it allowed him to fill up on the good stuff before having to eat salad. "I don't get it," he said, joining her.

"What don't you get?" she asked. "Your camp is happening!"

"But it's happening at Gabe's camp?" Zack asked. "Will I have to take classes and solve math problems and stuff?"

"No, I don't think so," his mom said. "They seemed to really stress in the e-mail that you'll be going to Camp Seneca, not Gabe's camp."

"But I'll *be* at Gabe's camp."

Zack's mom put down her fork and sighed. "The important thing is that they found a way to hold camp, despite the fire. Do you still want to go?"

Zack's answer came out without him even needing to think. "Duh."

"Okay, then. You're going! And you'll be in the same place as Gabe, so you'll have an automatic friend! Isn't that great?"

This did make Zack think, and he wasn't proud of his thoughts. What would it be like to be at Camp Seneca but on the same campground as the Smart Camp for Geeks and Eggheads? And more important, what would it be like trying to make friends at Camp Seneca when he had one particular geeky egghead hanging around, telling everyone they were brothers?

Chapter 6

GABE

Gabe's Clothes-for-Camp City was laid out all over his bed. He had done this last year, so now it felt like a tradition, but one he could improve upon every time. This year's city boasted a T-shirt skyscraper with blocks of color for different floors: blue on the bottom, then gray, then white, and on top, his neon-green Color War shirt from last summer, folded into a point. Mayor Gabe issued an ordinance that no building could be higher than T-shirt Tower, so his shorts were rolled and placed in a square around the tower to add architectural interest. He had two sweatshirt lakes, an underwear district, and a park made of balled-up socks. It was going to be hard to knock this city down.

His mom came into his room with his big suitcase. "Is the city ready for transport?" she asked.

"Let me warn the residents," Gabe said. "Attention, residents of Clothes-for-Camp City. The time has come for you to evacuate. The city will be moved to the suitcase for transport to camp tomorrow morning. I repeat, the city will now be moved to the suitcase and transported to camp."

"All right," his mom said. "What first?"

"The underwear district," Gabe said. He made his arm into a wrecking ball and swung it through, careful to avoid the shorts and shirts at the center of town. His mom sighed, and Gabe grinned. "Okay," he said. "From now on I'll transport without wrecking."

"Thank you."

The bed emptied as the suitcase filled up. "Maybe I can recreate the city in my bunk," Gabe said excitedly. "With Wesley and Nikhil's stuff, it could be a whole Clothes-for-Camp metropolis! Nikhil can make sure it's structurally sound."

"That sounds wonderful," his mom said. "Maybe you can add some of Zack's stuff, since he'll be there too."

"Yeah," Gabe said, trying to still sound excited. "But

Zack won't be in my bunk," he reminded her, and himself.

When Gabe had first seen the e-mail about SCGE sharing their campground with Camp Seneca, he'd wished he hadn't tried so hard to make Mission: Campossible a success. When he finally found the nerve to call Zack, they both said the obligatory happy things about sharing the campground, but Gabe found himself reverting back to a year ago, when he was constantly trying to view things through Zack's eyes and worrying about what he saw. Gabe figured Zack would be angry that he'd have to share his first camp experience with a bunch of nerds, and his voice, if not his words, confirmed it. Gabe wouldn't dare tell Zack about Clothes-for-Camp City, especially a structurally sound Clothes-for-Camp metropolis. So what would it be like with Zack, and other kids like him, at SCGE all summer long?

"Okay, how about your other bag?" Gabe's mom said. "Are your toiletries in there?"

"Yeah, I just have to add my toothbrush in the morning."

"What about your school supplies?"

"Check."

"Spare pair of glasses? Goggles?

"Check and check times two."

"What are we missing?"

Gabe looked over the packing list and mentally confirmed that each of the items was packed. "Nothing," he said. All that was missing was his previous certainty that camp would be fun.

Chapter 7

ZACK

The camp packing list said to bring eight T-shirts, and Zack had already chosen seven. He stared at his drawer, trying to decide which should be his eighth. The gray one with the blue wave that wrapped around the side was pretty cool, but so was the navy one he'd caught from a T-shirt cannon at a Rangers game.

The apartment buzzer rang, startling him, but he still couldn't decide on a shirt. His mother poked her head in the door. Her shoulder dropped when she saw his open suitcase, empty but for seven carefully chosen T-shirts. "Gabe is here, and Chad's bringing the car around. I take it you're not ready."

"It's only eight forty-five," Zack pointed out. "You said we're not leaving until nine."

"Well, Gabe's here already, and I doubt Chad can find a parking spot. Let's move it along." She disappeared again, and Zack knew he'd better be done by the time she came back. Now he realized he probably should have accepted her offer to help him pack last night, or at least should have started earlier than ten minutes ago.

He looked back at the packing list. It suggested bringing five pairs of shorts. He stared at his shorts drawer for an entire minute before he heard his mom's footsteps, snapped out of it, and decided to forget the list. He picked up all his shorts in one big blob and dropped them into the suitcase. Moving like he was in a time-lapse segment on TV, he added all his swim-suits, a beach towel, two pairs of flip-flops, and an extra pair of sneakers. The suitcase was already filled way above the top, but Zack didn't stop to worry about how he'd close it. He added a handful of socks and a couple of pajama shirts. What else?

His mom came back in and raised one eyebrow at his suitcase. "Did you pack your bathroom stuff yet?" she asked.

Bathroom stuff! "No, can you get it? Don't forget my hair gel!"

Zack spotted his iPod on his bed. That was extra important;

38

it shouldn't go in his suitcase. He put it in his school backpack along with his cell phone, camera, and baseball-card binders. "Ah!" he said, spotting his cell-phone charger sticking out of the wall. He unplugged it and added it to the backpack.

His mother reappeared with his shampoo, conditioner, toothpaste, and toothbrush in a plastic bag. He saw that she'd also added a stick of deodorant that she must have bought, but he didn't have time to be embarrassed about the fact that his mom had been thinking about his armpits smelling.

She sighed at his overloaded suitcase. "It'd fit better if you folded things."

"Hair gel?" Zack asked.

"I forgot." She left and returned with the hair gel and an added comb.

"Throw it in, Mom," Zack said. "I think I'm all set."

"Were you using the packing list?" she asked. She looked around the room for it, but Zack's rushed packing had only made his room messier than usual.

"I didn't need it," Zack said. "If I forgot anything, you can mail it to me."

"Do you have some warm clothes? I think it gets cool at night up in the woods."

"Good idea," Zack said, snapping. He put his favorite hoodie in the suitcase.

The buzzer sounded twice, which meant Chad was waiting outside with the car.

"Let's zip it up," said Zack's mom. "Why do I have a feeling I'll be at the post office tomorrow?"

Zack laughed. "How could I need *more* stuff? This thing won't even close." The suitcase was so jammed that he couldn't get the top anywhere near the zipper. He moved some things around so there was less of a big mound in the middle, but he still was far from being able to close it. His mom moved the bag of toiletries to a front compartment. That helped, but not much. Her cell phone rang, and it was Chad asking when they were coming down and reporting that Gabe had a sleeping bag with him.

"Gabe has a sleeping bag," Zack's mom relayed. "Do you need to bring one?"

"I don't know," Zack said with a shrug. He took an armful of clothes and moved it to his backpack. Then he put on the sweatshirt. His mom sat on the suitcase, and Zack was able to get the zipper closed, though the seam looked like it might split.

"There," Zack said. "No worries."

His mom shook her head. "No worries," she repeated, pulling Zack in for a hug.

"Mom!" he said. "We have to go."

Zack put his backpack on, even though it felt weird since it was round with clothes. His mom rolled the suitcase out of the apartment and down the hall. "Sleeping bag!" she remembered, after hitting the elevator button.

Zack dropped his backpack, ran back to the apartment, and returned with his sleeping bag.

His mom was holding the elevator door for him. "Oh Zack," she said when he got inside. "I'm going to miss you."

"Mo-om," Zack said, stepping away. It wasn't a long elevator ride, and he didn't want to be caught hugging his mother when it opened on the ground floor. She started to sniffle, which he hoped was because she'd miss him and not because she was upset that he wasn't hugging her. And then it really hit him that he wasn't going to see her for six weeks.

There probably wouldn't be anybody downstairs but Gabe.

Zack put down his sleeping bag and wrapped his arms tightly around his mom. "I'm going to miss you, too."

41

Chapter 8

GABE

Gabe fell asleep as soon as the car hit the highway. He'd been so anxious about camp that he'd barely slept the night before, and with Zack occupied by his phone at the start of the drive, Gabe didn't fight the urge to drift off. He woke up when they were about halfway there, but at that point Zack was asleep and so was Carla, so Gabe chatted with his dad for a while. Then, in anticipation of his Heroes class, he began reading his copy of *The Odyssey* and was taken in by the story of the cunning warrior trying desperately to get home. Wanting to save the bulk of the book for the summer, Gabe stopped reading and looked out the window. Though he was technically traveling away from his house, Summer Center was in many ways another home, and he pretended to be Odysseus, sailing through storms and outwitting enemies to return to the people he loved. As they got closer to camp, a faint smell of smoke drifted into the car, and large chunks of the woods seemed to be missing. Gabe wondered how Odysseus would react if he returned home to find a forest fire had consumed half of the trees.

Gabe's heart rate picked up when he saw the sign saying to TURN HERE FOR THE SUMMER CENTER FOR GIFTED ENRICHMENT. "We're here!" he shouted. Forget Odysseus; Nikhil would be here! And Wesley, and Amanda!

Underneath the SCGE sign was a handwritten one on cardboard adding AND CAMP SENECA! Gabe looked over at Zack, who managed to look cool even when he was asleep— his head rested easily against the window, his mouth was closed without a hint of drool, his headphones were hanging from his ears—and he thought, Zack's here too, and he will be all summer.

He was still excited, and he wanted Zack to be too, so he poked his arm. When Zack didn't move, Gabe shook him until he did. "We're here!" he said again.

Zack blinked a few times and then yawned. He looked out the window and then back at Gabe. "Dude," he said, offering his fist to Gabe for a bump. "We're here."

"You go to the left, Dad," Gabe said. "That's where the camp office is, where you register and find out your bunk."

But Gabe's dad slowed down and rolled down his window to talk to a teenage girl who was standing in the road. "Good morning!" she said. "Are you here for Summer Center or Camp Seneca?"

"One of each, actually."

The girl peered in the window and smiled. "Summer Center is registering in the camp office over to the left here, but Camp Seneca is registering in the athletic building, which is on the other side of the campground, to your right." She handed a map through the window, which Gabe thought was unnecessary, since he knew the campground as well as his own house.

"Where should we park, then?" Gabe's dad asked.

"You probably have a lot to carry, so I would pick one camper to register first, and park there. Then drive around to the other registration area."

Gabe's dad turned around to face the boys. "Who wants to go first?"

Gabe did a mental cost-benefit analysis. He was curious to see the Camp Seneca setup, but he was also anxious to get registered and find his bunk. Zack spoke up before Gabe decided. "We can do Gabe first," he said.

Gabe's dad looked at Gabe for confirmation, and Gabe shrugged. *Is it because he doesn't want me to come to his registration?* he wondered.

"Summer Center wins," Gabe's dad said to the girl. She pointed him to the left, and he thanked her before driving on.

Everything looked just like Gabe remembered, and he had to show his dad everything, and he saw what he thought was Wesley's car, and before he knew it, he was bouncing up and down in his seat like a little kid. He kept his hand poised over the belt buckle so he could press it the moment they parked. When they did, he jumped out of the car and took a deep breath of camp air, which made him wrinkle his nose. Last year, camp smelled like the perfect combination of trees, cafeteria grease, and new textbooks. This year, it smelled like burnt toast.

"What's that smell?" Zack asked.

"It must be from the fires," Carla said.

"It doesn't usually smell like this," Gabe said. "It smelled

45

great last year, remember, Zack?" He was glad Zack had come to pick him up last summer, even though it meant he'd discovered that it was actually a nerd camp. Since Zack had been there before, at least he knew it didn't always smell bad.

"Hi, Gabe Phillips."

Oh no. Gabe knew Amanda Wisznewski's voice and poke without having to turn around, and even though he was, in a weird way, looking forward to seeing her, this was definitely not on the track of introducing his family to the best SCGE had to offer. He turned around, ready to see the girl who'd spent all last summer following him around but insisting that it was Gabe who was following *her* around. "Hi," he said.

The girl behind him wasn't who he expected. It was Amanda, but she looked different. Her hair wasn't as long or as puffy as Gabe remembered. It was shoulder length and smooth and—how would he describe it?—*silky.* Instead of sticking out of her head in a triangle, it fell straight down and seemed to bounce around. She had new glasses, too. Narrow purple ones made of titanium. She was wearing her blue Color War shirt from last summer, but the sleeves were rolled up and the bottom was knotted right above her shorts. She looked, Gabe thought with surprise, good.

"Why are you looking at me like that?" Amanda asked. "You look weird."

Gabe didn't know how he was looking, but he tried to reset his face to look normal. "Your hair looks different," he said.

Amanda sighed, like she was tired of having people point it out. "Yeah, I got it blown out yesterday."

Gabe didn't know what that meant, and he wanted to stop talking about her hair anyway, so he changed the subject. "Have you registered yet?"

Amanda held up her registration packet. "I'm in bunk 3A. I know you won't compare classes, since you wouldn't tell me online what you're taking. But I'm sure we'll be together if it's meant to be." Amanda looked to Gabe's side. "Is this your stepbrother? The one who was here last year when you saw the eastern milk snake?"

Zack stood taller at this, and Gabe nodded. "Yeah," he said. "Zack. Zack, this is Amanda."

"Hey," Zack said, lifting his chin to her. "I'm going to Camp Seneca."

"They're registering in the athletic building," Amanda said.

"Yeah," said Zack.

47

"Are you ready to go in, Gabe?" his dad asked.

"Yeah," Gabe said. He wondered if he was supposed to introduce Amanda to his dad and Carla, but before he could make up his mind, Amanda walked up to his dad and held out her hand.

"I'm Amanda Wisznewski," she said, "Gabe's best friend."

Gabe's dad smiled and glanced at Gabe, who was shaking his head and turning bright red. "Nice to meet you, Amanda."

"You must be Gabe's stepmom," Amanda said to Carla, as though she'd just realized why Carla looked different from Gabe's mother, who'd come to pick him up last summer. "I'm Amanda Wisznewski."

"Yes, we've heard a lot about you," Carla said.

Gabe pressed his eyes closed behind his glasses—*but not because we're best friends!* he wanted to shout—and when he opened them, Amanda was looking at him with a knowing smile. "We're going to go register now," he said to her. "See you later."

Amanda kept smiling. "Bye, Gabe." She spun around, her silky hair bouncing, and galloped down the hill toward the cabins.

Gabe needed a positive encounter after that one, and he got it in the form of short, wiry Wesley Fan, who was waiting to register. "That's Wesley!" he said as his family joined the back of the line.

Wesley turned upon hearing his name, and his mouth dropped open. "Gabe!" he called. "My favorite Geek! Or are you Egghead?"

Gabe ran up to him, partly to give him a hug and partly to make him be a bit quieter with their nerdy nicknames. Zack had seen the caricature of Gabe and his bunkmates with the label *Smarty, Geek, and Egghead,* but who knew if he remembered it, or if there were other Camp Seneca kids around? There were going to be Camp Seneca kids around all summer.

"Hi!" Gabe said.

Wesley jumped and threw his arms around him, knocking Gabe over and almost taking down his own mother in the process. Gabe laughed as he got up. He was glad to see that Wesley looked exactly the same as he remembered. It didn't even seem like he'd gotten any taller, but he must have, because Gabe had, and Wesley still came up to his nose.

"Are you Geek or Egghead?" Wesley asked. "I don't remember."

"Geek," Gabe said, "because my name starts with *G*. Nikhil is Smarty, and *you're* Egghead."

"I am?"

"Yeah. Because Nikhil pointed out that your head's shaped like an egg."

"Oh yeah!" Then Wesley got serious. "Is it?"

"Kind of," Gabe admitted.

They both laughed.

"I can't believe I went a whole year without remembering that I am Egghead," Wesley said. "Nikhil said he's bringing the drawing so we can put it on our wall. We'd better be in the same bunk again."

"We'll find out soon," Gabe said. He pointed to the registration desk, where a counselor was motioning Wesley forward.

Gabe went back to his family while Wesley registered. "Wesley's hilarious. He forgot his own nickname," he told them, shaking his head.

"I thought you guys were supposed to be smart," Zack said.

"Ha," Gabe said, but it felt like he'd been slapped.

"Zack," Carla warned.

"I'm joking around, Mom."

"It's okay," Gabe said. He stared straight ahead and wondered why that comment had stung. Did he want Zack to think he and his friends were smart, or didn't he? It would be so much easier if Zack were his real brother instead of just a stepbrother he'd met a year ago. Real siblings *had* to like you no matter what, and genetics made it more likely that you'd be similar anyway. It wasn't fair that Gabe had to always feel self-conscious around someone who was supposed to be his family.

But then he rethought and made a mental observation that he'd have to record later: He didn't *always* feel self-conscious; he usually felt comfortable enough around Zack. It was being at camp—the place where Gabe was supposed to be in his element—that brought back all the worry and unease in full force. And since the Summer Center staff were allowing Camp Seneca to share their campground, he had to spend his whole summer this way. Now *that* wasn't fair.

Wesley skipped over to Gabe, holding his registration packet above his head like it had been handed down from the heavens. "Bunk 3B!" he sang. "I'm in bunk 3B, and I asked if you and Nikhil are in it, and they said—wait, do you want it *three be* a surprise?" Wesley snorted.

"No, tell me," Gabe said.

Zack rolled his eyes, just getting Wesley's pun.

51

"Okay. You're in 3B too! I mean you're in 3B *also*, not 3B-number-2. I don't even know if there are bunks with numbers like that." Wesley thought.

"I don't think there are," Gabe said.

"I don't think so either. Anyway, we're all together!"

"Yes!" Gabe said, happy and relieved. At least some things would be the way they were supposed to (three) be.

Chapter 9

ZACK

"Is it just me," Zack said to his mom, "or did Gabe get even nerdier in the past fifteen minutes?"

"Shh," his mom said, smiling. They were standing outside bunk 3B. Gabe and his dad were inside dropping off Gabe's stuff.

Zack glanced behind him, making sure Gabe hadn't come outside and heard. He'd seen the way Gabe had recoiled at his crack about being smart. He felt terrible about it, yet here he was making fun of him again. It was as if he had a nervous tick, like that girl at the skate park who chewed on her hair at the top of the half-pipe.

Zack wished he knew how to act around people who were so much smarter than him. Last year, when he'd come to pick up Gabe from camp on the last day, being at SCGE was like landing on another planet. (And if the rulers took one look at his report card, they'd stick him on the first shuttle back.) Zack didn't *want* to live on Planet Geek and spend his summer in school, but standing here now, outside an SCGE bunk, he wondered if anyone passing might mistake him for one of the smart kids, or if it was obvious that he didn't belong.

"Gabe's in his element here," his mom said. "It's nice to see. Imagine what you and your friends must seem like to him."

Zack gave her a cheesy smile. "Normal?"

His mom rolled her eyes. "When I go pick you up from the skate park, I barely recognize you. I can't understand a thing you boys say."

"What do you mean?" Zack asked.

His mom put on a deep voice and started moving her hands like she was a robot. "Yo, dude," she grunted. "Let's rip it slammin'!"

"Mom!" Zack looked around frantically and put out his hands to stop whatever it was she was doing. "What was *that*?"

"That's you with your skateboard friends."

"We do *not* sound like that. Or look like that. No one does." He shook his head. "Dude."

His mom once again moved like she was sawing the air with a stiff arm. "Dude. Whatevs yo!" she said gruffly.

A few kids were passing by and casting sideways looks at her. Zack wondered if the term "die of embarrassment" was based on actual incidents, and if he'd be the next casualty. He took two giant steps away and stuck his headphones in his ears. His mom laughed and gave him a hug. He tried unsuccessfully to push her away.

Chad came out of Gabe's cabin, rubbing his hands together. "We'll see Gabe later to say good-bye. You ready to go over to your end of the camp, Zack?" he asked.

"As long as Mom stops acting like a freak."

She kissed Zack's forehead. "Is Gabe all settled? I want to see his bunk." Zack waited outside while she went in. He figured he'd see Gabe's bunk at some point; right now he was anxious to get to his own. If, like his mom said, Gabe was in his element here, would Zack be in his element on the other side of the campground? *Do I even have an element?* he wondered. He put on his headphones to block out his nerves.

When she came out, the three of them walked back to the car and drove around to the athletic building, where a big, hand-painted billboard welcomed them to Camp Seneca. Zack couldn't put his finger on what, exactly, was different, but entering the gym made his whole body relax. Like the Summer Center office, the gym had teenagers directing traffic, college students working the registration desks, and lines of kids with their parents, but the atmosphere was just . . . cooler. *I think this is my element,* he thought, his lips spreading and curling up. Thankfully, his mom knew better than to try her skateboard slang here.

Zack found out he was in bunk 5C, also called Tomahawk. From the way the girl at the next registration desk glanced over with curiosity when the counselor said it, Zack knew Tomahawk was a good bunk to be in. He, his mom, and Chad made their way to the cabin, which was on the opposite side of the big field from Gabe's, closer, Zack knew, to the lake. The cabin was long and narrow but made up of separate "rooms" without doors. Each room had two sets of bunk beds, except for the very first room, which was smaller and had only one bed for the counselor. Zack found his name on a bed in the second room, alongside beds marked *Ryan*, *Abbot*, and

Thunder, which he thought was the coolest name he'd ever heard. There was another guy in the room with his parents, but Zack couldn't tell which one he was, and a third made his way in with his dad, which made it hard for anyone to move.

Within a couple of minutes, though, all the parents cleared out to go to parent meetings—there was one for SCGE parents at the same time, so Zack's mom and Chad were going to split up—and the space became much more breathable with just the three boys.

"Shot top bunk!" one of them said, putting his hand on the top right bunk.

The other kid, who had ear-length blond hair that he had to keep pushing away from his eyes, tried to call the other top bunk, but Zack was quicker.

"Shoot," said the blond guy. "Guess I'm on the bottom. Thunder, too." He laughed. "He's going to be pissed."

"You know him?" Zack asked.

"Yeah," the blond guy said. "He was in my bunk last year. This your first summer?"

"Yeah," Zack said. "I'm Zack."

"Abbot." He pushed his hair off his forehead and then held out his hand for a fist bump. "You Ryan?" Abbot asked the other boy, whose dark hair was in such a short buzz cut, it was like the two of them had been asked to demonstrate opposites.

"Yeah," said Ryan, bouncing on his top bunk as though testing the mattress springs. "You can call me RJ, though."

"Cool," said Abbot.

"Were the bunks like this at Camp Seneca?" Zack asked Abbot.

"They weren't all split up like this. Like, it was just one big room with fifteen guys. But this is okay, I guess. At least we don't have to bunk with the nerds."

"What do you mean?" RJ asked.

"This camp we're at," Abbot said. "Summer Camp for Gifted Education or something? It's for nerdy kids. They take tests or something all summer."

"No way," said RJ.

"It's true," Zack said. "They take a test to get in, and then at camp they take classes, like in school. My stepbrother goes to it." He wanted to get out the truth—that his stepbrother was one of them—as soon as he could. Trying to hide it was going to be impossible, so his best bet was to put it out there from the start and to act like it was no big deal.

Abbot laughed, but then stopped when he looked at Zack and realized he wasn't joking. "Serious?" he asked. "Sorry."

"It's okay," Zack said with a shrug. "He knows he's a nerd. They know people call it Smart Camp for Geeks and Eggheads."

"Ha," said RJ. "Smart Camp for Geeks and Eggheads. I thought this was just another regular camp."

"Nope," said Zack. "But at least we have our own bunks."

"At least the nerd's not your *real* brother," Abbot added with a laugh.

RJ said, "Heh," and Zack smiled uneasily, his heart pounding. *You don't even know Gabe,* Zack thought. *What difference does it make to you if he's my real brother or not?* He wanted to punch Abbot in the nose. But he also wanted to start off on a good note with his bunkmates, and punching one of them— one who'd been there last summer and was probably friends with a lot of the others—wasn't the way to do that. Letting the comment slide wasn't a good idea either; he had to say something. "Dude," Zack said, trying to sound serious but easygoing.

"Just kidding," Abbot said. He grinned and tapped Zack's arm.

"You better be." Zack tapped Abbot back, but not as hard as he would have liked.

Chapter 10

GABE

Gabe stretched himself out along a bottom bunk bed, keeping his feet at the edge of the mattress and seeing how far his fingers could reach. He imagined Wesley above him, twisting and talking in his sleep, and Nikhil across the way, his clothes for the next day neatly folded on the floor next to him. He heard someone enter the room and sat up quickly to see which of his friends it was, but instead he saw a short boy who was round in every way: his shape, his face, his bowl-like haircut, and his red glasses frames.

"Hi!" Gabe said, smiling. "I'm Gabe."

The boy nodded but didn't say anything. He smiled a

little, but mostly he just looked around the small space.

"Are you in this part of the bunk?" Gabe asked.

The boy looked at him and nodded so slightly that Gabe wondered if he really saw it. It had been so crowded with families when Gabe arrived in the cabin that he had just spotted his own name on the doorway; he hadn't even checked that he was with Wesley and Nikhil, though he knew they could probably switch around if they weren't placed together. Now he edged past the silent, chubby boy to look. There was his own name, and Wesley's, and Nikhil's—*yes!*—but also a fourth: Dong Dong. Was that really a name—*this* guy's name?—or had some Seneca campers gotten here early and written it as some sort of joke?

"Are you Dong?" Gabe asked hesitantly.

The boy nodded again, more perceptibly this time, and seemed to become happier.

"Where are you from?" Gabe asked.

"Seoul," Dong replied.

"In Korea?" Gabe said. That would explain his name. "Do you live in America now?"

Dong shook his head. "Korea."

"You just came here for camp?" Gabe asked, impressed.

61

Dong gave what Gabe was starting to recognize as his signature small nod. "S-C-G-E," he said, pronouncing each letter carefully.

Gabe knew there were some campers who came from other countries, but he hadn't met any last summer. Now he'd have one living in his bunk. How cool was that?

"Excuse me," said a voice, and Dong took a step into the room.

Nikhil appeared behind him. He was a full head taller than Dong, and his hair stuck straight up, making the height difference even more pronounced. "You probably want to move out of the way even more, if you can," Nikhil said, pointing to the big trunk he was dragging. "I don't want to accidentally hurt you."

"Nikhil!" Gabe cried. He ran past Dong and gave Nikhil a big hug, pushing them both into the trunk.

Nikhil stood up and straightened his shirt. "Gabe!" he said. "Do you smell that? It's a good thing I packed these, just in case there's lingering contamination." He reached into his backpack and pulled out a paper surgical mask. Then he put it over his head so it covered his mouth and nose, like he was going to clean Gabe's teeth. "Don't worry. I brought enough for you and Wesley," he said, the words muffled by the mask. "I'm so glad we're all together again! I mean, I'm sure I'd be able to get along with different bunkmates, but you know." "Yes," Gabe said, glad to see Nikhil hadn't changed. He still liked to play things as safe as ever. "It wouldn't be the same without all three of us." He stepped aside and motioned to their new bunkmate. "Plus Dong."

Nikhil looked at Dong, and Gabe could almost see the gears turning inside his head, putting together the round boy's presence with the name on the doorway. After a few seconds of processing, Nikhil pulled the mask down so it covered his neck rather than his mouth, and he held out his hand for Dong to shake. "Hi, I'm Nikhil. Don't worry. I've got enough masks for you, too."

Dong shook Nikhil's hand and gave his small nod. At that moment, Wesley burst through the doorway and tackled Nikhil. Dong fell onto a bottom bed, and Gabe barely jumped out of the way in time.

"The whole gang is back together!" Wesley sang, stretching out the last word into a full scale of operatic notes.

"The whole gang," Nikhil said, "plus Dong."

"Dong!" Wesley said with a chuckle. He stood up,

straightened his thin black glasses, and grinned. "Right. There aren't any empty beds this summer because there's got to be room for those Seneca people." He paused briefly when he noticed the doctor's mask hanging from Nikhil's neck, but then he went back to Dong. "I saw your name on the doorway. Is your last name Dong too?"

Dong nodded.

Gabe sat down on one of the bottom beds. "And your first name is Dong."

Dong nodded again.

"Do you have a middle name?" Nikhil asked, sitting on the other bottom bunk.

Gabe thought he saw Dong's mouth turn up at one corner as he said, "Dong."

"So your name is Dong Dong Dong?" Wesley said. His mouth dropped open. "That is awesome!"

"Really awesome," Gabe agreed.

"But some people in America might not think so," Wesley said.

Nikhil looked relieved. "It doesn't exactly have the best connotation here."

"I think you need a nickname," Gabe said.

Dong didn't say anything, and even though Gabe scrutinized his face, he couldn't tell if Dong liked that idea or not.

"How about Triple D," Wesley said.

"Tri-D," Nikhil tried.

"D-cubed," Wesley said.

"3-D!" Gabe said.

Dong's eyes ping-ponged from one bunkmate to the next, but not even that last suggestion made them light up.

Wesley cocked his head and moved his lips back and forth. "Dong Dong Dong," he said, his eyes narrowing in thought.

Nikhil chuckled. "It sounds like an old clock striking three."

"That's it!" Wesley announced. "Three O'Clock!"

Gabe cracked up. "Three O'Clock. Do you like that nickname, Dong? Be honest."

Dong raised his shoulders. Then he gave the smallest of small nods.

Wesley patted him on the back. "Great to have you in our bunk, Three O'Clock."

Nikhil shook his head but smiled. "Welcome aboard."

Chapter 11

ZACK

Zack and his bunkmates were supposed to unpack while their parents were at the meeting, but Zack promptly stopped when he discovered two things: There were no electrical outlets in the bunk for his phone charger, and RJ had also brought a binder full of baseball cards. At first, Abbot showed no interest in the cards; he didn't know anyone who collected them, and he preferred to complain about the lack of outlets, which he said all the cabins at the real Camp Seneca had. But as Zack and RJ started making trades and talking about how much some of their cards were worth, he started asking more questions and getting into it. Zack and

RJ started teaching Abbot about collecting, and before they knew it, it was time to meet their parents in the cafeteria for lunch and good-byes.

Zack's stepdad gave him a firm handshake, and his mom managed to hold herself together, which Zack appreciated, even though she wouldn't have been the only one crying. One girl was loudly sobbing into her mom's shoulder, and one dad bawled and hugged his son, who stood there stoically (pretending he was invisible, Zack figured).

The parents filed out, but the campers stayed in the cafeteria for a meeting. First, the director of SCGE introduced herself and welcomed them to their campground. When she was done, the head of Camp Seneca jumped on top of a cafeteria table and shouted into a microphone, "Helllooooo, Camp Seneca!" A whole bunch of campers started screaming and pounding on the tables with their fists, Abbot included. Zack and RJ looked at each other, then joined in.

The director pointed to someone off in a corner, who turned on music that rang through the cafeteria, drowning out the pounding. The director started dancing right there on top of the table, and all the counselors jumped up and started dancing too. Zack looked around in wonder, laughing and nodding to the beat. Some of older campers joined in, and all the girls, who were on the other side of the cafeteria, began cheering and clapping along. Zack's counselor, Marco, climbed between Zack and Abbot and then did a moonwalk across their whole table. That got the whole room cheering even louder.

The music faded out, and the director, beaming, signaled for everyone to sit down. Zack looked around at the cafeteria full of kids and counselors—and no parents—grinning and laughing, some still moving to the fading music. No wonder Gabe loved camp so much.

The director laid down some camp rules. Listen to your counselors. Stay with your group, and go where you're supposed to go on time. No leaving your bunk after lights-out. Be safe. Be nice to one another. "And be nice to the SCGE campground and its campers," he said. "We're *their* guests. When you get back to your bunks, your counselors will be giving you maps of the campground that show our areas, their areas, and shared areas. Imagine your parents invited some distant cousins to stay at your house, and when they came, they trashed your living room and started going through your stuff without asking. Not cool, right? So let's be good guests, stay in our part of the camp, respect the shared areas, and let them do their own thing in their own space."

"Like we'd want to have anything to do with them anyway," Abbot whispered to RJ. RJ put one finger to his lips and motioned with his head toward Zack. Not wanting to ruin the moment, Zack pretended not to hear or notice.

"And most important," the director said, "remember to have fun. This may be a different campground than you're used to, but this is still Camp Seneca. Get ready for the best summer of your life!"

Zack cheered and pounded the table like everyone else. He was ready.

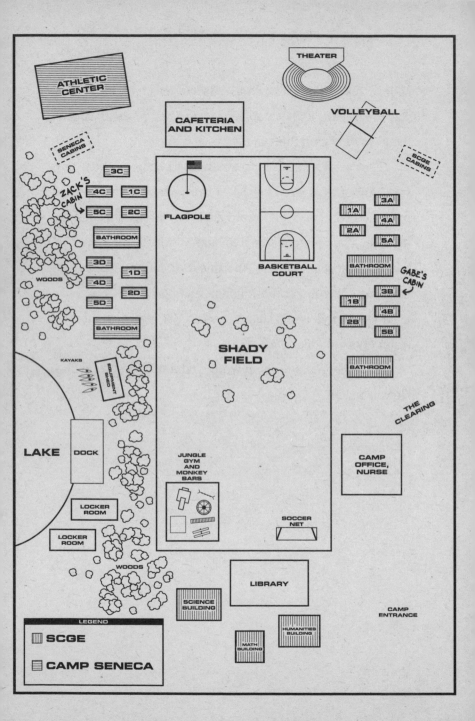

Chapter 12

GABE

The music pulsed through the cafeteria doors, making Gabe's feet vibrate in his sneakers. "What are they doing in there?" Gabe said. "Are they eating lunch or having a dance party?"

"Maybe it's both," said Wesley. "And all the food is dancing too." He snorted. "I bet bananas would be good dancers."

"Bananas?" said Gabe. "No way. They'd slip on their peels."

"Fair point," said Wesley. "How about chicken legs? They'd be good dancers. Just picture it."

Nikhil, picturing it, wrinkled his forehead. "Maybe the counselors should go in there, just in case. Someone could slip, or choke."

"They must have their own counselors," Wesley said. "What do you think, Three O'Clock? Would you go to a food disco?"

Three O'Clock stared at him for a few seconds, then nodded.

The doors burst open, the music increased exponentially, and a rush of Camp Seneca kids came barreling through, talking and shouting. The SCGE counselors moved their campers aside so they wouldn't get trampled. Gabe watched with wonder and dread. How could he tell, just by watching these kids stream by, that they were more like Zack than like him and his bunkmates? Was it their hair? The way they were laughing? The lack of buttons on their watches? Whatever it was, it made Gabe glad his glasses had new lenses, the kind that looked regular even though they were bifocals. He was also relieved that they'd convinced Nikhil they didn't need the masks to go to the cafeteria. From the way all the SCGE campers got quiet when the Seneca kids came parading past, Gabe guessed he wasn't the only one who was self-conscious.

Gabe caught sight of Zack in the mob. He was talking excitedly to the kid next to him, not looking at any of the SCGE campers. Just behind him was a boy with shaggy blond hair that hung into his eyes. He smirked as he passed, and said, loud enough for the boys from bunk 3B to hear, "Later, nerds!"

Wesley looked like someone had thrown a bucket of ice water on him. "Did he just say what I thought he said?"

Nikhil shook his head sadly. "Perfect. This place is supposed to *not* be like school. Well, it's supposed to be the fun, learning part of school, but not the annoying, mean-people part of school."

The Camp Seneca parade ended, and all the SCGE campers began filing into the cafeteria for their lunch.

"*We're* sharing *our* camp with them," Wesley said as they found their bunk's table. "They could at least be nice to us."

"I know!" Gabe said. He sat down so hard that it hurt his butt, but he didn't care. That kid's insult validated his fear about having to share their campground. "It's totally unfair."

"Doesn't your brother go to Camp Seneca?" Wesley said to Gabe. "Maybe he can be our ally there."

"Maybe," Gabe said. But even Three O'Clock looked doubtful.

Chapter 13

ZACK

"Shoot." Zack stared at his empty suitcase. Maybe he should have packed earlier than this morning. And maybe he should have unpacked before his mom left. He went to call her, but his phone had no signal. "Shoot," he said again.

"What'd you forget?" RJ asked.

Zack smirked. "Underwear."

RJ's mouth dropped open. Zack noticed for the first time that he had braces. Maybe braces weren't so bad if you didn't also wear glasses and T-shirts that said things like ALL-STAR READER.

Abbot cracked up. "No way," he said.

"Way," said Zack, "Maybe I should have looked at the camp packing list."

"Thunder forgot shorts last year," Abbot said, referring to their fourth bunkmate, who still hadn't arrived. "He wore the same pair for three days before our counselor realized and gave him shorts to borrow."

"Did they fit?" RJ asked.

"No," Abbot said with a snicker. "We were playing flag football, and someone went to pull his flag, and he pulled the shorts all the way down. It was hilarious. Guys kept trying to pants him all summer after that. Good thing Thunder didn't forget to bring underwear too!"

"Ugh!" said RJ. "Then he'd be wearing the counselor's shorts with no underwear."

"Going commando," Abbot declared, "is not good in flag football."

Zack laughed until he realized that without any underwear, he'd have to "go commando," and what if they were going to play flag football, or any other sport? It'd be even worse if there were girls around.

He could wear today's underwear tomorrow, and then he could turn it inside out to wear the next day and *maybe* the day after that. How long would it take if his mom mailed him more?

"Are you going to borrow underwear from Marco?" RJ asked.

Abbot pretended to throw up. "Don't even think about trying to borrow from me. That's gross."

"Yeah, me neither," said RJ.

"Dude," said Zack. "You think I want to wear someone else's underwear?"

"I borrowed my cousin's underwear once," said Abbot, "after we went in his pool. But that's okay because he's family."

"Yeah," said RJ. "It's probably okay if it's family."

Family! Zack thought. *Gabe!* He didn't love the idea of wearing Gabe's underwear, but it was better than wearing the counselor's or going without. And Gabe was right across the field in another cabin. Maybe he wouldn't even have to borrow underwear. Gabe and his friends were so smart, they could probably figure out a way to make boxers out of pillowcases and paper clips or something. "I've got to go see my brother," Zack said.

"I thought you said he was your stepbrother," said Abbot.

"Yeah, whatever," Zack said. "I can borrow from him,

or he can help me figure something out. He's really smart like that."

"Right," said Abbot. "He's at nerd camp."

"We're not supposed to go to that side of the camp," RJ said. "We're not even supposed to leave the bunk until three."

"I'll ask Marco," Zack said. "He should let me if I tell him why."

RJ and Abbot followed Zack to the front of the cabin to look for their counselor. But his section of the cabin was empty, as was the area right outside.

Zack looked across the field to where the SCGE cabins were. It was so close; he'd be back in five minutes. "I'm just going to go," he said. "If Marco comes back, tell him I went to the bathroom or something."

RJ furrowed his dark eyebrows, but Abbot nodded, impressed. "I'll come with you," he said. "I want to see their bunks."

Zack thought it'd be easier to go by himself; he was less likely to be caught. He also didn't want Abbot to meet Gabe or Gabe's bunkmates. Last summer, the walls of Gabe's bunk were covered in math problems and pictures of presidents or other old guys. If Abbot saw that, he'd blab about it all summer.

And if Gabe tried to create underwear out of notebook paper and duct tape, Abbot would make fun of him for life. "I saw his bunk last year," Zack said. "They're the same as ours."

Abbot shrugged, making it clear that he was going to come anyway. "You coming, RJ?"

RJ squinted as he looked across the field. "Nah," he said. "I'll stay here and cover for you guys in case Marco comes back."

Zack looked straight ahead as he and Abbot jogged across the field. He wished it were the other way around, and that RJ was with him instead. Even though it had only been a few hours, he could already tell that he liked RJ more than Abbot. He hoped that he liked Thunder, if he ever came. Guys like Abbot were always worse in groups. Living with two of them would feel like living with ten.

All the camp staff were walking with purpose, so no one stopped Zack or Abbot as they crossed the field and found bunk 3B. The counselor was there, but Zack just said he was Gabe's brother and needed to ask him something, and the counselor led them through the cabin without asking any questions himself.

Once there, Zack sighed; it was even worse than he'd

feared. Gabe and another guy were holding a big map of the world up against the wall, while a third held up a ruler, measuring. The fourth sat on a bottom bunk bed, punching numbers into a big calculator. All of them were wearing dentist masks. When Gabe saw Zack, he pulled his mask quickly over his head. He was wearing his night brace underneath, with baseball cards slid under the strap, just like he'd demonstrated back in Zack's room.

Zack heard Abbot inhale sharply, and for the second time that day, he wondered if he might die instantly of humiliation. He was embarrassed at being related to Gabe, but he was even more embarrassed *for* Gabe, who looked like he wanted to crawl underneath the bed until lights-out.

"Hey," Gabe said, his face a deep purple.

"Sorry to bother you guys." Zack hoped his voice conveyed how much he meant it, and that Gabe and his friends remembered that he was sorry once Abbot opened his mouth, since Zack was sure he would say something obnoxious. "I'm Gabe's stepbrother, Zack, and this is"—he hesitated, not wanting to say *my friend*—"Abbot."

The chubby kid on the bed just stared at him through his round glasses. The tall, dark-skinned guy gripped his ruler tightly and looked warily at Abbot. The one who Zack remembered meeting at Gabe's registration—*William? Wallace? Wesley!*—gave a goofy smile and said, "Greetings. What brings you to Nerdland?"

Abbot snickered, and Gabe and Zack both winced. *Keep it cool*, Zack thought. *Just play it easy.* "Thanks," he said, motioning with his chin to Wesley. "It's actually kind of embarrassing. I, uh, forgot to pack underwear, and I thought Gabe might have some I could borrow."

"Zack!" said Gabe. His night brace stretched as he grinned. "You forgot to pack *underwear*?"

Zack chuckled. "Yeah."

Abbot shook his head. "What a moron, right?"

"Well," said the boy holding the ruler, who was still wearing his dentist mask, "it's difficult to remember everything. That's why I always make my own packing list to cross-reference with the list camp supplies. And then I tape a copy of each on the inside of my suitcase to check before zipping it up, just to be safe." He paused. "I guess it's a little late for that now."

Abbot jabbed Zack with his elbow. Wesley snorted.

"Did you pack any bathing suits?" Gabe asked.

"Yeah," said Zack. "Four or five."

"You can wear those until your mom can send you underwear."

"Oh yeah!" said Zack. "I knew you'd think of something smart like that."

Gabe grinned. "But I have some you can borrow, too. They're new," he said, rummaging through a drawer of one of the small dressers. "My mom took them out of the package to sew in this label with my name on it, but then I actually put them back in."

New underwear! Zack thought. This was even better than he could have hoped. It was worth coming here, despite the embarrassment.

"Here they are!" Gabe announced. He held up the package and then handed it to Zack.

The chubby boy on the bed started to giggle, seeming only now to understand what Zack needed.

"Tighty–whities," Abbot said, grabbing the package. Once in his hands, he squinted at it. "What's on here?"

At first Zack thought maybe something was stuck to the plastic, like a piece of gum. But when he took it back and looked closely, he saw what Abbot was talking about.

This wasn't just white underwear; they had some sort of design.

"Dinosaurs," Gabe said, blushing again. "Real ones," he added. "Not, like, cartoony ones. I think they're to scale, actually."

Zack resisted the urge to slap his forehead. This was just so Gabe.

Wesley pushed his way through the room, which was difficult with so many people there. "Can I see?" he asked excitedly. "I'm taking the paleontology class." He took the package from Zack's hand, and his mouth dropped open. "These are so cool!"

Abbot's eyebrows raised so high that they disappeared behind his hair.

Gabe laughed nervously. "Do you need anything else?" he asked Zack.

"No, that's it," Zack said. "Thanks for these"—he held up the dinosaur underwear—"and for the bathing suit suggestion. I'll wear my bathing suits first."

"Why?" said Abbot. "I'm sure everyone in our bunk will love these super cool briefs."

Zack tried to apologize to Gabe with his eyes. "Come

on, man," he said to Abbot. "Let's get back before we get in trouble."

"Yeah," said Abbot. "You nerds had better get back to decorating your classroom. It doesn't look geeky enough yet."

"Come *on*," Zack said again. He gripped the underwear in one hand, grabbed Abbot's arm with the other, and made his way out of the cabin without saying good-bye.

Chapter 14

GABE

The minute Zack and Abbot left, Gabe sank onto Nikhil's bottom bed.

"What on the-third-planet-from-the-sun was that about?" Wesley said.

"He need Gabe's underpants," Three O'Clock explained.

"I got *that*," Wesley said. "I meant, how dare they come into our territory?"

"Yeah," said Nikhil. "The director said we have to stay on the SCGE part of the campus, and Camp Seneca isn't allowed here. Didn't they get copies of the map?"

"Gabe's stepbrother coming here is one thing," Wesley

said, pacing the area between the beds and waving his finger for emphasis. "But to bring that other guy with him. The one who made fun of us by the cafeteria."

"I know." Gabe took off his glasses and pressed his palms into his eyes. "I'm so sorry, guys. This is terrible!"

"Terrible squared," Wesley agreed. "It was bad by the cafeteria. But our bunk is *our bunk*. It's supposed to be a safe zone."

"Terrible cubed." Nikhil pulled out a copy of the camp map that their counselor had given them. "Our bunk should be neutral, like Switzerland in both world wars."

"I think the whole campground should be neutral," Gabe said, "with everyone respecting everyone. But our bunk should be *our* area." He pointed to Nikhil's map, on which the SCGE areas were marked by vertical stripes and the Camp Seneca areas were marked by horizontal ones.

"Right!" said Wesley. He ripped off a piece of tape and stuck the map on the wall. Pointing to the neutral, white parts of the map, which signified shared zones, he took a pencil from his pocket and added *SWITZERLAND* to the legend. Then he used the pencil like a pointer for his briefing. "The whole campground is Switzerland, and our bunk

85

is Allied territory, where we can measure for our maps and practice our digits of pi and wear our dinosaur underwear. And they can stay in *their* bunks, where they can . . . do whatever it is they like to do, and do it without even *bringing* underwear."

They all stood around looking at the map and one another, indignant. But then Nikhil sighed and sat down on his bed. "I guess even the Allies had to worry about invasion."

Gabe sat down next to him. "Yeah, and that was the bombing of Pearl Harbor."

Wesley took his pencil and drew horizontal stripes through bunk 3B, turning Nikhil's campus map into a war playbook, a record of boundaries redrawn and regions lost and won.

They sat in silence, no longer excited to hang their room decorations or perfect their Color War algorithm or even protect themselves from inhaling toxic fire fumes. Summer Center was supposed to be about the brazen pursuit of academic happiness, but not even hanging out in their bunk was safe. Which meant not even hanging out in their bunk was fun.

* * *

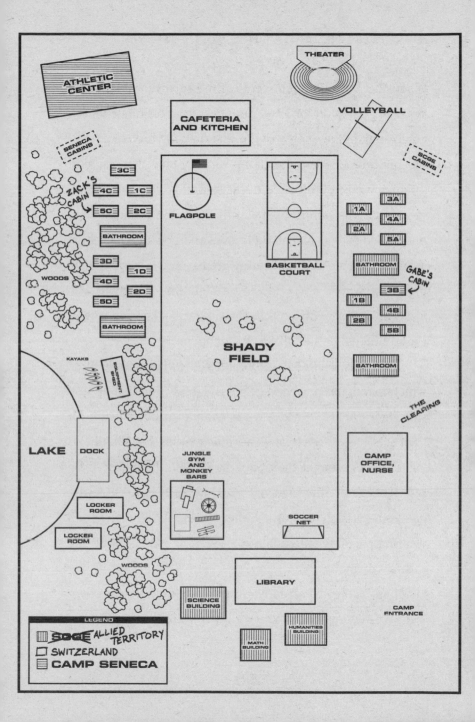

When the wake-up siren went off the next morning, Gabe kept his glasses off for a full minute so that his other senses could soak in the energy of the first day: the breaking light, the buzzing cicadas, the damp air so chilly that his skin prickled against the fleece of his sleeping bag. It was summer, and it was camp, and it was the first day of school, all at once. He'd be learning about heroes and research methods, swimming in the lake and eating greasy cafeteria food, playing in the woods and choosing a nighttime activity. It was a day so full of promise that the anxiety of sharing it with Camp Seneca seemed like a distant memory.

SCGE was slated to eat breakfast before Camp Seneca, which meant the boys had to dress quickly and line up outside their cabin. They'd have a chance to come back for their school supplies before morning classes, but Nikhil and some others brought their backpacks with them, just to be safe. They walked in big clumps along the field to get to the cafeteria, passing the Camp Seneca campers, who were still wearing pajamas but gathered outside in some sort of flag raising ceremony.

"I guess they've already claimed the field as their own too," Wesley muttered, "since they're raising their flag."

Gabe kept his gaze straight ahead, determined to not let Camp Seneca ruin his day.

When he got to the cafeteria, he slid his tray down the line, filling his plate with stiff pancakes and rubbery scrambled eggs. He skipped the oatmeal, which he distinctly remembered made him feel queasy last year, no matter how much lemon juice he squeezed on it to kill potential bacteria. He settled at a table with his bunkmates, noticing that Three O'Clock's plate had only one piece of toast and a single slice of tomato, and wondering if he was nervous or homesick. Everyone was away from home—it shouldn't matter, in theory, that Gabe's parents were a few hours away while Three O'Clock's were on the other side of the world, but Gabe knew that in actuality it would.

"The food is safe here," Nikhil said to Three O'Clock, "even though it may not look like it. No one got really sick last year, at least."

Three O'Clock nodded but didn't get up to get more food. He just continued nibbling on his toast.

"Don't look!" said Wesley. Gabe and Nikhil both stopped eating and looked. There was Amanda Wisznewski, walking right past their table. She had two bowls of cereal, one on either end of her tray for balance. Her hair was still silky, but more frazzled than it had been yesterday, probably from having been slept on. She was walking with Jenny Chin, who was so tall now; she must have grown six inches over the school year. She held her tray with one hand and pointed at Gabe with the other, then whispered something to Amanda. The two of them settled at a table far from the boys but within their direct line of sight. Gabe didn't realize he was still staring at them until Amanda waved at him, which made him look away quickly.

"That's Amanda Wisznewski," Nikhil told Three O'Clock. "She loves Gabe."

"No she doesn't," Gabe said. He took a big gulp of orange juice; his cheeks felt hot.

"Is she in both of your classes again?" Nikhil asked Gabe.

"I don't know," Gabe said. "I purposely didn't tell her what I was taking. But probably."

Wesley nodded knowingly. "I bet she called the camp to ask. People in love do crazy things. My older brother started wearing a fedora because this girl he liked worked in a hat store."

"She's not in love," Gabe said to Three O'Clock.

The four of them all looked at Amanda's table. She stopped talking to Jenny and smiled at them. And then, without any warning, she blew Gabe a kiss.

Chapter 15

ZACK

Zack wasn't hungry. Last night he'd loaded up on pizza at dinner, then s'mores at the campfire, then candy in the bunk, so his stomach was still maxed out. And the breakfast food didn't look particularly appetizing. Yet he still stuffed himself with pancakes, eggs, bacon, oatmeal, toast, and a bowl of Fruit Loops, for a healthy component. He usually ate like this—until he felt like bursting—only when the food was extra spectacular, or when he was nervous about something. He couldn't even pretend that this food was spectacular, so it must have been that he was nervous.

It had been so strange to wake up in his cabin, across from RJ. He remembered the way it felt to wake up in his New

York apartment for the first time and realize that he wasn't at a sleepover or on vacation. The walls were the wrong color and the pillow was too hard, but it had still seemed like *he* was the one out of place, not the room. Here at camp, it felt like he was the same, but the surroundings were all wrong. He'd never raised a flag in his pajamas at either of his homes, or—thankfully—had to clean his room for inspection before being allowed to eat breakfast. His mom wasn't there, and neither was his dad. Gabe was though. Zack had caught a glimpse of him coming out of the cafeteria as the Camp Seneca kids went in, and it had reassured him. If Gabe could do this, Zack certainly could too. That thought made him calm enough to not eat the pancakes he'd piled on his plate. They were chewier than pancakes should be, anyway.

"Listen up, Tomahawks!" Marco shouted. He pounded on the table four times with his fist, making the plates rattle and the juice splash out of any full cups. "After breakfast this week, we have swimming, so we'll be going back to the cabin to get bathing suits and towels. But after swimming, you'll split up and go to activities you pick. You'll have another activity session this afternoon. I'm passing around a list of options." He held up a piece of paper. "Next to your name, mark your first choice and your second choice for both morning and afternoon. We'll try our best to make sure everyone gets his first choice, but no guarantees, so make sure you like your second choice too. Choose wisely, because you'll be doing these activities every day this week. Any questions?"

"What if we don't get what we want?" RJ asked.

"I think the bigger problem will be deciding which you want most," Marco said. "There are some awesome options. But remember, you'll get to do all this stuff with Tomahawk at some point. And we're here six weeks, so you'll have time to try everything."

Zack waited for the paper to come around to his part of the table.

"I hope they have good choices," Abbot said, his mouth full of sausage.

"Dude," said Zack, "I don't need to see your half-chewed food."

"You sure?" Abbot said. He stuck out his tongue, and a stream of sausage bits fell onto the table.

"Oh gross," said RJ.

Abbot snickered, which made him choke on the rest of the sausage, which made Zack and RJ laugh.

The sign-up sheet made its way to RJ, and Zack and Abbot kneeled on their chairs to look at it too.

Morning activities	Afternoon activities
Archery	Fishing
Hiking	Cooking
Ultimate frisbee	Book club
Arts & crafts	Martial arts
Table tennis	Friendship bracelets
Music	and lanyard/gimp
Volleyball	Nature survival skills
Snorkeling	Drama
	Soccer

"Lame," said Abbot. "All the good ones are missing because we're not at the real Camp Seneca."

"Well, we're not at the real Camp Seneca," RJ said.

Zack gave RJ a smile of approval. He was getting fed up with all of Abbot's complaining. At least Marco had reported this morning that Thunder wasn't going to come to camp after all. Abbot had other friends in Tomahawk, but Zack was glad he wouldn't have to put up with two complainers in his room.

Zack asked RJ if he could see the list. "These choices look pretty good to me."

"They're okay," Abbot said. "But there's no skate park or ropes course. Those were the best ones."

Ignoring him, Zack said, "I'm going to do nature survival skills in the afternoon. Maybe I'll be like that guy on TV who can live in the woods for, like, a month, eating bark and drinking bear blood."

"Gross!" said RJ. "I'm going to do that too!"

Zack marked nature survival skills as his and RJ's first choice. He noticed that a few other guys from Tomahawk had put it as their first choice too, so he put a star next to it for himself and RJ, hoping that'd make it clear that they *really* wanted it. He chose fishing as his second choice for the afternoon. He was tempted by soccer, which RJ put as his second choice and Abbot put as his first, but he figured he could play soccer at home. It was hard to fish in New York City.

Then he looked more closely at the morning options. "What's archery?" he said.

"Bows and arrows," Abbot said. He stretched one arm straight forward and bent another back, then he threw a hard-boiled egg with his back hand as though he were shooting it from a bow. It landed on the seat next to Zack, who tossed it back onto Abbot's tray.

"Snorkeling," said RJ. "That's kind of like scuba diving, right?"

"Yeah," said Zack. "Me and my dad went snorkeling in Malibu. It's pretty cool."

"I think I'm going to do that," RJ said.

"Put me down for archery," Abbot said. "I want to see if the setup here is any good."

Zack marked it down, somewhat annoyed because he'd wanted to try archery, but he didn't want to commit himself to spending more time with Abbot. He decided to go for ultimate frisbee, with snorkeling as his second choice.

As soon his group got to the lake for their morning swim time, though, he hoped he didn't end up snorkeling. It was only nine in the morning, which meant the air hadn't warmed up yet, let alone the water. The campers stood by the dock with their towels wrapped around them like blankets while one of the lifeguards gave a water-safety lesson. The lifeguard finished, leaving them twenty minutes to swim, but a cold wind blew off the lake, rustling the leaves in the woods around them and making everyone clutch his or her towel tighter.

The girls broke into groups and started talking, a few brave ones dipping a toe into the water before shrieking and pulling it back out. The boys stood around, daring one another to jump in.

"This blows," Abbot said, pulling his towel over his head like a nun. "At Camp Seneca, our swim time was in the afternoon, when it was actually warm out. And there was a heated pool!"

Zack and RJ exchanged tired looks. "We're not at Camp Seneca," Zack said. "Get over it."

"It was so much better than this place," Abbot whined. "I bet Thunder decided not to come because he knew this would suck. It's cold and boring, and there are all these nerds here."

"There aren't any nerds here right now," RJ said.

"Yeah," said Zack. "I think they're in school."

"Just knowing they're around makes this place lame," Abbot said.

Zack walked onto the dock. The lake looked cold, but skinny-dipping at the north pole would be more fun than listening to Abbot for another second. "You know what's lame?" Zack said. "Standing around and complaining instead of swimming."

"Dude," said Abbot, joining him on the dock. "It's, like, five degrees out. And there are probably nerdfish in there."

Zack thought about the early mornings he'd gone surfing with his dad. Before he moved to New York, he spent every other weekend at his dad's apartment, and they'd often wake up on Monday mornings while it was still dark so they could catch some last waves before Zack had to go to school and say good-bye for two weeks. They'd arrive at the beach when the sun was just rising, but there were always a few hardcore surfers already there, and some of them would wave at Zack like they were old friends. Even with a wetsuit on, that first punch of cold water would make Zack wish he'd slept in. But the rush of riding his first wave always made him glad his dad had gotten him up. Now that he didn't live near his dad anymore, he was especially glad he hadn't wasted those mornings sleeping.

He dropped his towel. "I'm going in."

"All right!" said RJ.

"You're coming in too."

RJ froze. "I am?"

"If you want," Zack said. "But *you're* definitely coming in." He grabbed Abbot's arm, and—quickly enough to catch

Abbot off guard—launched himself into the air. Abbot tried desperately to get out of his grip, but RJ was behind him, pushing. Abbot managed to drop his towel at the tip of dock before the three of them hit the water.

The coldness of the water startled Zack, and his skin exploded with pinpricks. But Marco and his Tomahawk bunkmates were cheering, and some of the girls were watching and giggling. He pumped his fist in the air. "Come on!" he shouted to the shore. "It's not so bad once you're in!"

"That's a lie!" RJ yelled. "It's freezing!"

Zack laughed and dunked himself under the icy water again. He came out and splashed close to Abbot with a gasp. "Look out!" he said.

Abbot, his long hair dripping and his body shivering, opened his eyes wide. "What?"

Zack pointed in the water. "I almost got bit by a nerdfish!"

RJ cracked up, and he and Zack splashed around happily until swim time was over and their lips were a deep blue.

Chapter 16

GABE

"I knew it!" Amanda said. "I *knew* you'd take Research Methods too!"

"How did you know?" Gabe asked, shaking his head.

Amanda smiled mysteriously and sat down next to him. Gabe took out a binder and pen, wondering if she really did call the camp to ask which classes he was in. Or maybe certain people simply liked to learn about the same things, since there were a few other kids in the room who had taken Logical Reasoning with him and Amanda last summer. The principles of logic could console him now. Just because they were in the same class again didn't mean, like Amanda always said, that he and those other kids were "meant to be," or that any of them were in love with him. All it meant was that they were all going to learn about research methods—different approaches to doing every kind of experiment—and it was going to be fun.

But what did it mean, after lunch and recess, that Amanda was also in Heroes of Our World and Imaginations? Gabe tried not to think about it and instead tried to appreciate that the only other person he knew in that class was Mr. Justice, the teacher. He'd had Mr. Justice for Poetry Writing last summer, and he was happy to see that he was as warm and soft-spoken as Gabe remembered. He had new glasses that looked like they were made of wood, his long dreadlocks were tied back at the bottom of his neck, and he gave Gabe a high five when he walked into the room. "Are you ready to be heroic?" Mr. Justice asked him.

Gabe shrugged and said, "I guess so."

Mr. Justice chuckled and patted him on the back.

"I'm ready to be heroic," Amanda volunteered.

"That a girl," said Mr. Justice. He clapped his hands once. "Take a seat, everyone! We've got lots of learning to do." He kept the lights off in the room to create an atmosphere of serenity, but said he'd turn them on if it was so serene that people started falling asleep. "I don't think you'll fall asleep in here, though. The title of this class is Heroes of Our World and Imaginations. Over the next six weeks, we're going to learn about real heroes from history around the world: people like Dr. Martin Luther King Jr., and Mahatma Gandhi, and General Custer. We'll talk about fictional heroes too, from literature and movies. I'm talking about Odysseus. Harry Potter. Katniss Everdeen."

"Batman!" a girl shouted.

"Yes!" said Mr. Justice. "Comic-book superheroes! We'll talk about them, too."

The girl and another next to her looked at each other and hissed, "Yes!"

"And we'll talk about everyday heroes," Mr. Justice continued. "Who are some everyday heroes?"

"Firefighters?" a boy guessed.

Mr. Justice nodded. "Who else?"

"That pilot who landed on water," someone said.

"Soldiers," said the girl who liked Batman.

"Lawyers," Amanda added. Gabe resisted rolling his eyes. He knew that Amanda's dad was a lawyer. But that did give him an idea.

"Our parents," Gabe said.

"Right on," said Mr. Justice. "And by the end of this summer, all of *you*. As we study these heroes and talk about what makes them heroic, you should all be striving to be everyday heroes, if not ones who will go down in history. You are going to do three big projects this summer. One will involve a real hero from history. One will be creating your own fictional hero. And the last one—the most important one—will be to do something heroic." Mr. Justice paused and let this sink in. He looked around the room and met everyone's eyes in turn, as though challenging each of them individually to take these words to heart.

A jolt of something electric surged through Gabe when Mr. Justice looked at him, like he was a robot who was just plugged in and brought to life. He could use every research method he learned in the morning to figure out how best to be a hero!

Gabe lifted his chin and returned Mr. Justice's brave stare. He was up for the challenge.

Chapter 17

ZACK

Zack was still shivering fifteen minutes after toweling off and changing into dry clothes. As he stood on the field, which was warming up as the sun beamed down in earnest, he was glad he'd gotten his first choice of ultimate frisbee for the morning. Poor RJ had to stick around the cold lake to snorkel.

Two counselors explained the rules of what they simply called "ultimate," then had everyone split into pairs with frisbees to practice throwing and catching before they started a game. Zack was about to ask the guy next to him if he wanted to partner when he felt a tap on his shoulder. He turned to see a girl with shoulder-length brown hair that had one small piece braided with purple and yellow string. She tucked that strand behind her ear, and Zack saw that she had a matching purple and yellow friendship bracelet around her wrist. "Want to partner?" she asked.

"Sure," Zack said.

The girl started jogging to an open part of the field, and Zack quickly caught up with her. "I'm Zack," he said.

"Lauren," she replied. "That was pretty cool how you just jumped in the lake before."

Zack grinned and shrugged. "I really just had to get my bunkmate in there. He was complaining too much about the cold."

Lauren stopped jogging and threw the frisbee to Zack. He was only a few feet away from her, but it bounced off his fingers and landed on the grass. Lauren laughed.

"Hey, I wasn't ready," Zack said. He picked it up, backed away a few feet, and threw it with a strong flick of his wrist. The frisbee sailed smoothly through the air—way over Lauren's head and to the right. *Shoot*, he thought as he watched her run to get it.

"Are you ready now?" she asked when she got back.

"Ready," Zack said. He hadn't thrown a frisbee in a long

time, and he'd never played ultimate before, but he was sure he should at least be able to catch it.

Lauren threw the frisbee with force and grace. It floated from her arm in a strong, direct line, right to Zack, and he caught it with ease. *Phew*, he thought. He threw it back, not nearly as well as she had, but at least it didn't go way off course this time.

"You must really like swimming," Lauren said as she tossed it again.

"What do you mean?" Zack asked.

"You changed out of your bathing suit and put on a new bathing suit."

Zack was glad he had to run to get the frisbee so Lauren wouldn't see him blush. "I really like surfing," he said when he got back. That was true, and better she think he wore board shorts all the time because he was a surfer rather than the real reason—that he'd forgotten to pack underwear. He prayed that his bathing suit wouldn't somehow fall down while playing ultimate. Good thing it wasn't flag football.

The counselors called them all to the center of the field. They split them into teams and handed out yellow and black jerseys. Lauren got black, so Zack tapped the guy next to him and asked to trade his yellow for a black. The guy shrugged and switched. "Hey," Zack called to Lauren, as they jogged down to the black team's side of the field. "Go black."

Lauren smiled. She had a dimple on one cheek. "Yeah," she said. "Go black!"

Zack was now completely thawed from his ice bath; if anything, he felt hot. He ran his heart out during the game and made sure to pass to Lauren, even a few times when other people were closer. Black ended up winning by two points, and he and Lauren were the first to high-five.

"What are you doing for your afternoon activity?" Lauren asked him as they handed in their jerseys.

"Nature survival skills, I hope," Zack said. "You?"

"Cooking. I'm psyched. I'm going to be a chef one day."

"Not a professional ultimate player?" Zack joked.

"Definitely a chef," she said. "Are you going to be a . . . nature survivor?"

The counselors called for everyone to line up and prepare to go back to their bunks.

Zack had an idea. "I might be a chef too. I put cooking as my second choice," he lied.

Lauren smiled. "Maybe I'll see you later, then."

"Yeah," Zack said, "maybe."

As soon as he got back to his bunk, he asked Marco if he could change his choices for afternoon activities.

"Too late," Marco said. "We already figured out who's doing what."

Zack's shoulders sank. "There's no way I can switch?"

Marco shook his head. "Why do you want to switch, anyway? Didn't you put a star next to your name for nature survival skills? So many people put that as their first choice, but I fought for you and RJ to get it." He squeezed his eyes shut, then opened them again. "I wasn't supposed to tell you that yet."

"I did want it," Zack said, picturing himself wearing a hat made of a dead squirrel. Would that impress Lauren? Probably not as much as preparing a delicious squirrel soufflé. "But now I want to do cooking. It's important."

"Cooking?" Marco said. "There's tons of space in cooking."

"So let me switch, then! And someone else who really wanted nature survival skills can have my spot."

Marco sighed. "You're lucky you have the world's best counselor, Zack. Let me see what I can do."

Chapter 18
GABE

The directors of Summer Center and Camp Seneca had clearly spent a lot of time figuring out schedules so that the two camps were in different parts of the campground at all times—except for five p.m. free time. The boys from bunk 3B were drying off from their three-thirty swim when their counselor told them that Camp Seneca would also have free time until dinner. Everyone groaned.

"Do they have to?" Wesley asked.

"You don't have to hang out with them," their counselor, Paul, said. "Just be aware that they're going to be out on the field or in the woods too. Be respectful."

"Tell that to them," Nikhil muttered into his towel.

Gabe, still fired up from his Heroes class, tried to take the higher ground. "I'm sure they're not all like that guy Abbot. Maybe some of them are nice, like Zack, and we'll make new friends."

Wesley snorted.

Gabe smiled halfheartedly. "Or maybe they'll just ignore us."

Nikhil wrinkled his forehead. "Maybe we should stay in our bunk until dinner, just to be safe."

"No!" said Wesley. "Three O'Clock and I want to listen for the birdcalls we learned about in Zoology. Right, Three?"

Three O'Clock looked at him for a few seconds, then blinked.

"Let's go to the woods, then," Gabe said, hoping he sounded heroic. "That's a shared area on the map, so it should be neutral."

But the woods were far from neutral. There were groups of Camp Seneca kids sitting on every picnic table. ("*On* the table!" Nikhil said, shaking his head. "That's really not safe.") They were walking like gymnasts on all the best logs and gathered in circles on the dirt, braiding lanyards or playing hand games. When the boys finally found a quiet spot to listen for birdcalls, a pack of Seneca kids came running through in a game of tag, screeching and howling and knocking Three O'Clock through the spiderweb they'd been hoping to study while listening for birds.

"Hey!" Wesley shouted after them. "We're trying to observe fauna here!"

The big pack of taggers didn't even hear him, but a smaller, slower group that was now passing through did, and they stopped and stared. "What?" one of the girls asked, trying not to laugh.

"Could you guys be careful?" Gabe asked. "We're trying to study animals."

"And not the human kind, like you," Wesley said, crossing his arms.

The Senecas looked at one another and snickered. "I told you they were nerds," one of the other girls said.

"Not the human kind," a boy said in a squeaky voice, trying to impersonate Wesley.

Wesley clenched his lips together, and Nikhil put his hand on his shoulder, just in case he was thinking of starting a fight.

The first group of taggers came running through again,

this time going the other way, and the girl who'd said they were nerds got tagged It. They all took off again, and Gabe had to jump backward to avoid being tackled. The boy who'd impersonated Wesley tripped as he ran, prompting Nikhil to say, "Watch out for gravity!"

Gabe's jaw dropped, Three O'Clock said, "Ha!" and Wesley said, "Go, Nikhil!"

The boy stared at Nikhil for a second. He rolled his eyes and repeated the line in that same bad impersonation. Then he ran off to share it with all of Camp Seneca.

By the next day at free time, not only did it seem like there were Seneca kids everywhere the SCGE kids wanted to be, but they were also all saying "watch out for gravity" in various fake accents before doubling over in laughter.

"Who cares?" Gabe said.

"Maybe they're repeating it because it was such a great line," Wesley said.

Three O'Clock put his hand on Nikhil's shoulder. Nikhil pushed it off. "I thought only you guys would hear," he said, "but I should have kept quiet, just to be safe."

A pack of Seneca girls walked past. One wearing short

shorts and oversize sunglasses sang, "Watch out for gravity!" over her shoulder. All her friends giggled and ran off.

Nikhil pressed his palms into his eyes. Wesley looked at his friend and stared after the girls, his fists clenched and his eyes narrowed.

By the third day of free time, some Seneca kids had started coupling "watch out for gravity" with a shove. They went out of their way to "accidentally" bump into an SCGE camper so they could say it. As the end of the first week neared, the taunt had evolved into Seneca kids pushing one another into an SCGE camper and shouting, "Watch out for nerds!"

Gabe began to dread five o'clock. The woods weren't safe, the field wasn't safe, and even being near the academic buildings meant risking being spotted by Seneca kids who'd make fun of you for wanting to be in school during free time. The SCGE kids started to hang out by their cabins, bored and glum and worried that anything they said might be overheard by someone from Camp Seneca who would turn it into the next camp-wide joke. Nikhil walked around with his shoulders hunched, and Wesley continued to seethe silently. Even Calvin Chin, C^2, the coolest guy at camp, seemed defeated. Gabe saw him hanging out by the upper boys' cabin, leaning against the wall as though he was there by choice.

Gabe was working up the nerve to go talk to him when a few Camp Seneca girls wandered by C^2, pointing and whispering. One of them blurted out, "Hi, C-circle!" Then they all shrieked and continued on their way.

C^2 rolled his eyes, but Gabe saw his lean become more of a slump.

"C-circle?" Gabe said, confused. "They think you're C-squared like the shape, not C to the second power?"

"I know, man," C^2 said. "What is happening to our camp?"

That night, Gabe and his bunkmates reshaded their map of the campground to reflect the current state of affairs. It was a saddening sight. Almost all of Switzerland, the area previously marked neutral, was now striped: Seneca-controlled land. Summer Center still controlled the academic buildings and most of their bunks, but the direction of the war was plain.

"We're not even one full week into camp," Wesley said, "and Camp Seneca has already claimed eighty-five to ninety percent of the territory. I don't even want Color War to break because they'll probably just claim that, too."

"It's true," Nikhil lamented. "They're advancing so quickly

that by the end of summer, we'll be written out of history."

Gabe wanted to remain optimistic, but it was hard to argue with the map; it had a clear legend, it was based on personal experience, and it was to scale—Nikhil had double-checked. Camp Seneca had conquered most of their land and, worse, their spirit. Even being in classes wasn't as much fun, given the prospect of running into Camp Seneca kids in between them. Gabe couldn't get excited about Research Methods, and he certainly didn't feel very heroic, having to hide out in his cabin. It was like the early days of meeting Zack, when he'd agonized over his every word.

Where *was* Zack, anyway? Gabe had only seen him twice all week, once outside the cafeteria when they were both in a rush, and once during free time, when Zack was sitting on top of the monkey bars, too busy talking to some girl to notice Gabe walk underneath. At least Zack wasn't one of the people shouting "watch out for nerds!" or making fun of C^2, as far as Gabe could tell. But it wasn't like Zack was crossing borders to defend Summer Center, either. Not that Gabe had expected he would.

"This summer sucks," Wesley declared.

Gabe stared at the map with a frown, wishing Wesley's declaration weren't true.

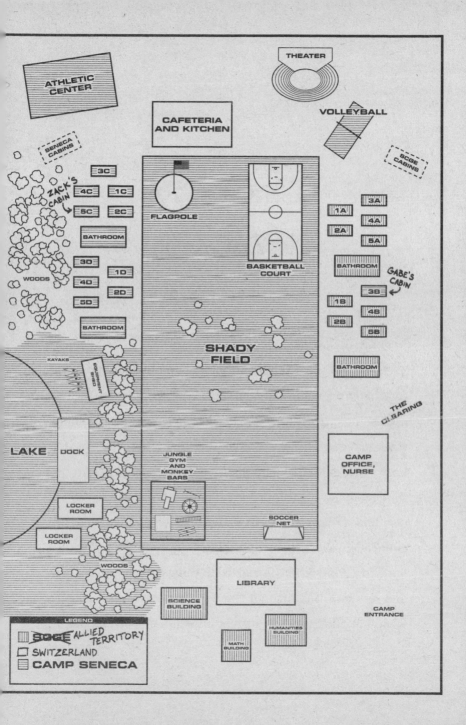

Chapter 19

ZACK

Zack was in love. When Abbot found out that Zack had switched from nature survival skills to cooking, he made kissy noises and chanted that Zack was in love with Lauren. But a week into camp, Zack didn't let that bother him. He was too busy being in love with cooking.

Cooking was so cool. For starters, it was easy. Someone else had already come up with all these recipes, and you could just follow them step-by-step. But cooking was also hard, in a good way. You had to cut things and measure them and mix stuff, and if you messed up, you could end up with something that was soft instead of solid, or burned instead of browned, or nice-looking but nasty-tasting. Cooking was dangerous, too. You got to wield a knife and throw things into hot oil, and if you used the wrong cutting board or didn't cook things thoroughly, you could kill someone with salmonella. Best of all, cooking was kind of like magic. You took all these boring ingredients, did stuff to them, and—presto!—produced something delicious. It was magic you could bite and swallow and brag about: *I made that happen.*

Zack could totally see why Lauren wanted to become a chef, and now it wasn't such a lie that he might want to be one too. Their cooking instructor, Zig, had goggle-like glasses and colorful tattoos that started at both of his wrists and disappeared into the rolled-up sleeves of his chef's coat. He left the campground before dinner to go work at a restaurant at a fancy resort in the woods, and he didn't come back until well after midnight. When Zack's cooking class started at three thirty, Zig's hair was either wet (from a three-fifteen shower) or completely disheveled, which signaled how late he'd worked the night before. He admitted that his real name was Ziggy, which left the whole class impressed with how he'd turned such a geeky name into such a slick one. Lauren and the other girls in the group were infatuated with Zig, but since

Zack was one of only two boys, the girls were totally into him and the other guy too. Just one more item for the growing list of reasons cooking rocked.

Zack also liked that Zig didn't treat his cooking protégés like babies. He didn't have them make Rice Krispie treats or cut sugar cookies into cute shapes topped with rainbow sprinkles. Instead he gave them big knives and spent most of the first day teaching them how to use them properly. He talked about acid and texture and master sauces, things Zack didn't know a thing about but was now anxious to understand. He and Lauren started hanging around the kitchen after the activity time ended at five, talking to Zig until the cafeteria staff kicked them out so they could get ready for dinner.

When Marco posted the sign-up sheet for next week's activities in the cabin, Zack was pumped to see cooking on the list again, as Zig had promised. "Put me down for cooking," he said to RJ, who was holding a chocolate bar in one hand and a pen in the other.

"Don't you want to do nature survival skills?" RJ said. "They taught us how to eat bark!"

"Dude, why would I want to eat bark when it only takes, like, forty minutes to make an awesome apple crisp?"

RJ stared at him with his eyebrows raised. Zack took a second to replay what he'd said in his mind, and then he started laughing. RJ grinned. "Okay, Betty Crocker," he said before taking a big bite of his chocolate bar.

"You should join cooking," Zack said. "Zig said after this next week, there's even going to be an advanced cooking choice for the people who keep coming back."

"That's okay," RJ said, swallowing. "I don't even like apples, crispy or not. I brought enough candy to make sure I don't need to eat a single apple all summer. If it runs out, I'm fine with bark."

Zack didn't bother explaining what an apple crisp was and why it was ten million times better than a crispy apple. Instead he put his hand out for a piece of RJ's chocolate bar, then popped it into his mouth. It was true that RJ had brought a whole summer's worth of chocolate bars, and Zack was glad he was willing to share. "Let's pick the same thing for the morning, then. Basketball? Woodworking?"

"How about archery?" RJ said. "Since Abbot already did it."

Abbot came into the cabin wiping sweat from his forehead using his shirt. "What about Abbot?" he asked.

"You already did archery," Zack said. "Are you going to do it again this week?"

"Nah. I already mastered it." He closed one eye and aimed an imaginary arrow. "I could hit a nerd from a hundred yards away."

Zack rolled his eyes. He took the pen and marked archery as his first choice, basketball as his second. Then he gave the pen back to RJ, who did the same.

"Whoops, sorry, man," Abbot said. He was always pretending to forget that Zack's stepbrother was an SCGE camper. "You don't care about watching out for nerds."

"I never even see them," Zack said, realizing it was true. "Marco said they have free time at five too, but it's not like they're around. It's just Seneca kids everywhere."

"Yeah," said RJ. "I think they're in their bunks or at the library."

"They're so weird," Abbot said, taking a bite out of RJ's chocolate bar—while RJ held it—without asking. "Remember when we went to your brother's bunk and they were all wearing dentist masks?" He snickered. "I told so many people about that."

"Yeah, yeah." Zack wondered, for the first time in a week,

what Gabe was up to. He did have to return the dinosaur underwear Gabe had loaned him, which he luckily didn't end up needing; he'd gotten by on bathing suits until a box arrived from his mom a couple of days ago. He didn't want to carry around a package of dinosaur underwear during free time, since he might not see Gabe. Maybe he'd go to Gabe's bunk again—without Abbot this time. It would be like at home, where he saw Gabe every other weekend. Thinking about it now, he missed Gabe. Gabe would definitely appreciate his newfound interest in cooking; he might even be able to teach him some smarty-pants science that could help him be a better chef.

He didn't know why he'd ever worried about being on the SCGE campground with Gabe. The two camps were completely separate, each doing its own thing. There weren't smart kids hiding behind trees, waiting to quiz Zack on his multiplication tables. Sure, some of the Camp Seneca kids joked about having nerds nearby, but it wasn't anything serious. Gabe had never come over to the Camp Seneca area, especially not to try to tag along with Zack. That must mean Gabe was happy, like Zack was, absorbed in his own bubble of summer-camp bliss.

Chapter 20

GABE

Gabe was miserable. His first big project in Research Methods was to conduct a survey to discover public opinion. The first bad news was that they had to work in pairs, and the second bad news was that Amanda claimed him as her partner. But the worst news of all was the results of their survey. Some pairs polled campers to find out their favorite and least favorite cafeteria choices, which recent technological advances they found most useful, or their most fascinating periods from history. Gabe and Amanda had boldly decided to gauge campers' feelings about sharing the campground with Camp Seneca.

They created their survey, passed photocopies around their bunks and the cafeteria, and even got permission to go cabin to cabin before lights-out to distribute surveys to the older and younger kids. After collecting and tallying the responses, they sat in Research Methods, the results spread across their pressed-together desks, and frowned.

How would you rate your feelings about sharing the SCGE campgrounds with Camp Seneca?

I love it!	3%
I like it.	1%
I'm indifferent.	3%
I don't like it.	19%
I hate it!	74%

How would you describe your interactions with Camp Seneca campers?

Very positive. Camp Seneca campers have been really nice!	5%
Positive. Camp Seneca campers have been fine.	15%
Neutral / I haven't had any interactions with Camp Seneca campers.	7%

Negative. Camp Seneca campers haven't always been nice.	44%
Very negative. Camp Seneca campers have been very mean.	29%

How does this summer at SCGE compare overall to your previous summers at SCGE so far?

This summer is much more fun!	0%
This summer is a little more fun.	5%
This summer is about the same.	8%
This summer is a little less fun.	12%
This summer is much less fun!	55%
This is my first summer at SCGE.	20%

"I think we need to present these results to the director of the camp," Amanda said. "She needs to see how unhappy everyone is."

"But what's she going to do?" Gabe said. "She can't kick Camp Seneca out. They already paid, and their campground got burned down."

Amanda tucked her pencil behind her ear. Because she'd swum and showered many times since that first day, her hair was no longer silky and smooth, but back to a puffy triangle. "She can tell their director to tell them not to be mean," she said, "so we can have fun at our own camp."

Gabe frowned with one side of his mouth. He was sure the Camp Seneca kids were getting the same speeches about respect that he and his bunkmates were. "Does that ever work?" he said. "They'd probably just make fun of us for telling on them."

Amanda's pencil slipped from her ear into her hair, and she ran her fingers through with increasing frustration, trying to find it. "Our survey results are practically unanimous. No one's having fun, and it's because of them."

"Well, we have to be able to find a way to make things better," Gabe said. "We can do experiments to see what works."

Amanda shook her head violently, but the pencil was still lost. "Our first experiment can be telling the director."

"But what can she *do*?" Gabe repeated, getting fed up with her pencil and her pessimism.

"Aah!" Amanda yelled. She slumped back in her chair and crossed her arms. The pencil slipped out, hit the floor, and rolled under the desk. She didn't move to get it. "I don't *care* what she does," Amanda said angrily, "but she has to do something. It shouldn't be *our* job to fix *them*."

That idea niggled Gabe's brain the rest of the morning and all through lunch. It seemed like Amanda was right, but Amanda *couldn't* be right. There had to be another approach.

He kept thinking about it during Heroes, when Mr. Justice gave a rousing account of the Battle of Little Bighorn. "Crazy Horse and the Lakota refused to succumb to the invaders," Mr. Justice said. "The Native Americans were outnumbered, but they fought bravely and smartly to defend their territory and their way of life."

Amanda, who Gabe could see was still grumpy, raised her hand. "Didn't the Native Americans lose in the end?" she said. "They won at Little Bighorn, but they still ended up losing, like, all of their land. Wouldn't it be stupid to fight if you know you can't win?"

"That's a good point," Mr. Justice said. "Sometimes you win the battle, but you don't win the war. What do you guys think, then? Is it still worth fighting the battle? Can you be a hero even if you lose?"

Gabe flipped to the front of his binder and scanned the

list of heroes Mr. Justice had given them. Some of them had won, and some of them had lost, but they all seemed to have one thing in common: They'd taken a stand. They'd tried.

And that's when it hit him. Amanda was right—okay, fine—but she was also wrong. As Summer Center campers, it wasn't their job to fix Camp Seneca. It was their job to fix themselves. They were never going to have fun if they kept letting Camp Seneca beat them down, if they hid in their bunks and moped about how unfair everything was. This was *their* campground, and being smart was their way of life. It was about time they started defending it.

He raised his hand. "It doesn't matter if you lose," Gabe said. "But you at least have to try to stand up for yourself."

That night for homework, Gabe formulated his ideas in a research proposal.

Problem: What will make SCGE fun again?
Hypothesis: SCGE will be fun if we don't let the
    Seneca kids run the campground.
Experiment: Stop hiding in our bunks. Stand up to Camp
    Seneca!

The problem was important, and the hypothesis was logical. The experiment was risky, but what did he really have to lose? SCGE-Seneca relations certainly couldn't get worse. Like Crazy Horse in the Battle of Little Bighorn, he was ready to act alone, but he knew he'd fare better if he had an army behind him.

Back in the cabin, he waited until all his bunkmates had brushed their teeth and changed into their pajamas. Then he stood, tall and strong, between the two sets of bunks. He cleared his throat. Three O'Clock put aside the letter he was writing, Nikhil placed a bookmark in his book, and Wesley finished attaching the rubber bands to his braces. Then Gabe began. "As you know, I've been studying our problem with Camp Seneca, and tonight I had a breakthrough in my research. I'm pretty sure I've hit upon a hypothesis worth testing, but I need your help."

Wesley nodded stoically. "Proceed."

"First of all," Gabe said, "a fun fact. Summer Center's initials are SC and Camp Seneca's are CS. They're our inverse, our exact opposite."

The boys nodded at one another, impressed.

"They're our inverse," Gabe repeated, "but not our superiors. We can't forget that this was originally our camp." He went on to tell them about the Battle of Little Bighorn and the brave Lakota who didn't back down, even if they lost in the very end. "We've been *letting* Camp Seneca take over our territory," Gabe explained, holding up the camp map. "Just letting them march in and take control, without so much as an attempt at defending ourselves."

"We're not supposed to fight," Nikhil said. "The campground is supposed to be neutral."

"Yeah, it's *supposed* to be," Gabe said, "but it's not. The Senecas are threatening our way of life. We can sit here and be miserable, or we can do something about it."

"You're right!" Wesley said, jumping up and bumping his head on the ceiling. "I'm okay!" he said with the same fire. "When the Japanese bombed Pearl Harbor, the US didn't just say, *Well, this sucks.* They declared war."

"War?" Nikhil jumped up too, careful to avoid the top bunk with his head. "People die in wars."

"Yeah!" said Wesley, raising a fist.

"What?" said Three O'Clock.

"No one's going to die," Gabe assured them. "I'm just saying we can't let Camp Seneca keep us from having fun. We have to assert our right to use the field and woods during free time."

"Right," said Wesley. He climbed down from his bed, squeezed next to Gabe, and put his arm around his shoulder. "Geek, you're a natural leader. Don't you agree, Three O'Clock?"

Three O'Clock gave a thumbs-up.

"Maybe we can try to have more fun *inside* our bunk," Nikhil suggested. "You know, just to be safe."

"Nah," Wesley said. "I'm tired of staying in here."

"But Nikhil's right," Gabe said. "It is risky. It'll be safer if we have more people with us. That's why countries have armies."

So they set about drafting theirs. They started with their own bunk, 3B. Wesley, Nikhil, and Three O'Clock stood behind Gabe in the next section of the cabin while he explained his hypothesis and requested help with the experiment. Those three boys then followed Gabe into the third section of the cabin to enlist the others. Section by section, Gabe became surer of his methods and more confident in his delivery. By the time they reached the front of the cabin, he imagined himself a great general, rousing his men for war. (A careful, casualty-free war, he assured Nikhil.) Of course Summer Center should take a stand! If everyone stuck together, of course they'd be triumphant! Gabe's mettle swelled in step with his army. Was this what it meant to be a hero?

* * *

The next morning at breakfast, Gabe shared the mission with Amanda and Jenny. They spread the word to their bunkmates, and to Jenny's brother, C^2. From there, the cause spread through the cafeteria as quickly as the wildfires that had created the Camp Seneca problem in the first place.

SCGE spirits were high. Everyone was fired up and ready to reclaim their land. Until five o'clock, when it was time to put the plan into action.

"What's the plan, exactly?" Nikhil asked. They were standing in front of their cabin, watching the Senecas running around the field.

"We hang out in the field or the woods," Wesley said.

Gabe nodded. "And we don't back down." His army was huddled in front of their respective bunks, waiting for someone—him, probably—to make the first move. Perhaps being a hero wasn't all it was cracked up to be. He surveyed the battlefield and imagined their opponents pushing them, laughing, and shouting "watch out for nerds!"

"How about we not back down tomorrow." Nikhil suggested.

Gabe frowned. Maybe he should go back into the cabin to gel his hair, or change into a plain T-shirt instead of his mathletes one. The Senecas would probably still find something to make fun of, and besides, he couldn't hide the nerdiness of his whole army.

What would Zack do? Gabe wondered, scanning the field for his stepbrother. Gabe couldn't spot him, but he knew the answer: Zack wouldn't bother changing anything about himself. He'd just walk out onto the field, confident and cool.

"This is *our* camp," Gabe reminded everyone, but mostly himself. He took a step forward. His friends followed. He took a few more steps. Then, after turning to make sure his friends were behind him, he sprinted onto the field.

They made it as far as the monkey bars before anyone from Camp Seneca realized. "Yo!" someone shouted. "Nerd alert!"

Gabe froze with one hand on the first bar. At the other end of the monkey bars was a Seneca, and not just any Seneca, but a boy who was built like a tank. "Excuse me," Gabe said to him, praying his voice wouldn't crack.

The boy grinned, like a dog baring its teeth. "Shouldn't you be in your nerd huts studying for a test or something?"

Gabe could sense all of SCGE watching him, waiting for him to be the leader he claimed to be last night. He looked at the tank. Those teeth could use braces. "No," he said. "It's free time."

"Yeah!" Wesley said, moving to stand next to Gabe. Since Gabe was ready to swing and Wesley was on the ground, he only came up to Gabe's waist. "He's going to swing across," Wesley said, "and an object in motion will stay in motion. So get out of my friend's way, or succumb to the laws of physics." Wesley stepped aside and held his arm out, inviting Gabe to go.

Gabe resisted the urge to apologize and instead began to swing across, the Seneca kid glaring at him. He didn't know what he'd do if the kid didn't move—Wesley conveniently left out the fact that an object in motion will stay in motion unless acted upon by a force—but a miraculous thing happened. Just as Gabe hit the halfway point, the boy broke his stare, mumbled "whatever," and walked away.

Gabe's eyes and mouth spread wide as he reached the other end. *It worked!* he thought. He wanted to whoop and squeal and do the chicken dance. *But what would Zack do?* he thought again. Zack would probably shrug and continue on his way, as though the whole encounter had bored him. So that's what Gabe did, only he also waved over his army from their cabins.

Summer Center kids stormed the field, and just like that, the battle was on.

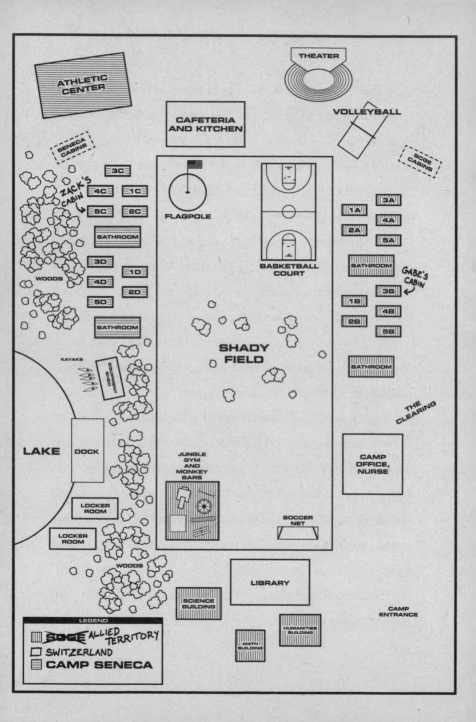

Chapter 21

ZACK

Zig had to jet right after the cooking session to get to the restaurant, so there was no reason for Zack to stick around the kitchen during five p.m. free time. He said good-bye to Lauren, then jogged back to his cabin to find RJ and grab his baseball-card binder. Cards were picking up in popularity at camp, and now that they'd been there long enough for packages to arrive from home, lots of kids were getting new packs, which made for increasingly good trading. Abbot even had his parents buy him a binder and stock it with cards. He'd gotten it at mail call that morning, and he was holding it proudly under his arm when Zack got to the room.

"You ready to be jealous of my cards?" Abbot said.

"Whatever you say, man." Zack took his binder from his drawer. "Where should we go?"

"The woods," RJ said. "A bunch of us traded at this good picnic table during free time the other day."

The three of them headed out of the cabin and into the woods. The campground seemed more crowded than usual. It hadn't even been two weeks, yet Zack already recognized all the Seneca faces. The kids who were saturating the campground now weren't the ones he was used to, though, and they weren't doing things he was used to, either. Some were throwing a frisbee, but they were shouting things about air resistance as they did it. One group was talking in old-timey language while holding styrofoam shields and swords. And when they arrived at the picnic table RJ had been thinking of, there was already a group of kids there trading cards. Zack and his bunkmates stood back, waiting for a good moment to ask if they could join. The traders, not noticing them, kept up their conversation. Zack didn't recognize any of the players they were talking about. He wondered if they had really old cards, or maybe ones that were for another sport.

"Come on," a girl at the table said to another. Her red hair was in not two, but three long braids. "Copper is *so* much rarer than boron."

"Don't listen to Serafina," a boy cautioned. "I got two coppers in one pack once, and no one in my whole school could find boron."

Abbot hadn't been trading long enough to really know the players, but Zack and RJ looked at each other in confusion. "What team does Copper player for?" RJ asked.

Everyone at the table turned to look at them. "What?" asked the boy who'd gotten two coppers in one pack.

"Copper," said Zack. "Is he good? What team does he play for?"

"What *team*?" the girl with three braids, Serafina, asked. "Metals, I guess."

"The Metals?" RJ said, his eyebrows close together. "Where are they from?"

"You mean, like, where are they mined?" another girl asked.

"No," said Serafina. "He probably means where on the periodic table. Copper's number 29. Period 4, group 11. See?" She slid the card out of her binder and passed it over to RJ. His face became only more confused as he looked at it.

Zack looked too. No wonder he didn't recognize the name

Copper; this wasn't a baseball card at all. The front just said "Cu" in big letters above the word "Copper," and had a bunch of numbers. The back listed the stats the girl had read (number, period, group), plus a "factoid": *American pennies were once made entirely of copper, but today they are mostly made of zinc that's coated with copper.*

"What kind of card is this?" Abbot asked, as though the card were made of slime.

"You've never seen Element Cards?" Serafina asked, incredulous. "*Everyone's* trading them. They each have one element, and you try to collect the whole periodic table."

"What's the periodic table?" RJ asked.

Every set of eyes at the table widened. Many of them were behind glasses, which only magnified the effect. "You're kidding, right?" said a boy with unruly black hair. "It's just the basis of all of chemistry."

"Chemistry?" Zack repeated. Now the periodic table sounded somewhat familiar, probably from talking to Gabe. That's when he realized. "You guys go to Summer Center, don't you?"

"Yeah."

Zack's cheeks flushed. They must have thought he was

so dumb for thinking copper was a baseball player.

"Nerd alert!" Abbot shouted.

Zack winced. The kids at the table crossed their arms or tightened their lips, but they didn't say anything.

"Get out of here," Abbot said. "Go to the library or something. This table's for trading baseball cards."

A couple of the kids started to close their binders, but Serafina didn't budge. She pulled two of her braids over one shoulder and the third over the other. "You guys go away," she said to Abbot. "Right now, this table's for trading Element Cards."

Right on, Zack thought.

"Yeah!" said the boy with wild hair. "Find somewhere else to trade your baseball cards. We were here first, so right now, this is the *periodic* table."

The other traders laughed, and one high-fived the boy who'd made what must have been a joke. Serafina snorted.

"Come on," Zack said. "We can find another place to trade."

"Here." RJ handed back the copper card. "If I were you," he said to the girl across from Serafina, "I wouldn't trade this for boring."

"You mean *boron*?" she said, breaking into a laugh. "It's true! Camp Seneca kids really are stupid."

RJ's eyebrows arched together again, this time out of hurt. Zack crossed his arms. They were right to claim the table, but they didn't have to be jerks about it. He opened his mouth to say so, but Abbot beat him to it.

"Shut up," Abbot said. "You nerds had better watch out."

Serafina shrugged. "Whatever." Then she turned back to the table and said, "So, what do you say? Your boron for my copper?"

The girl with the boron card glanced nervously at Abbot before replying. "I'll give you boron for copper, but I also want magnesium and one of the noble gases."

Zack wondered if they were speaking in some sort of smart-kid code language, and *magnesium* and *noble gases* really meant *let's attack these idiots with lightsabers.*

Zack put a hand on Abbot's shoulder. "Come on," he said. He and RJ started walking back toward the field. They passed lots of Summer Center campers on their way, some with binders of Element Cards, two passing binoculars back and forth, and three arguing over something involving a protractor.

Abbot stomped along, kicking a rock and leaving a trail of dust. "Who do they think they are," he grumbled, "telling us we can't use that table?"

"They were using it first," Zack pointed out.

"But they were using it for something dumb," Abbot said. "They're supposed to move when we tell them to. That's the way things worked until a few days ago, at least. And they called us stupid."

"Yeah, that wasn't cool," Zack agreed.

"Dude." RJ laughed. "They were trading science cards that have to do with *noble gas*. I don't think coolness is one of their strengths."

Zack laughed. That was for sure. But it was pretty impressive the way that girl had stood up to Abbot—he was glad somebody had. Maybe the nerds weren't cool, but it seemed they did have some strength. He hoped Gabe wasn't letting himself be pushed around either. He also hoped he wasn't going around talking about *noble gas*. "Noble gas," he said aloud, shaking his head.

"Yeah," said Abbot. "I'll show you noble gas." He stopped walking, scrunched up his face, and let out a loud, juicy fart.

Chapter 22

GABE

At every meal, kids stopped by Gabe's table to report their stands against Camp Seneca. With every report, every success, every free time, the camp was growing more confident. Gabe could see it in his fellow campers' faces, hear the pride in their voices, and feel the energy returning to Summer Center.

A few days after the resurgence began, a platoon of younger kids found Gabe in the cafeteria at dinner and shared the latest triumph.

"We were trading Element Cards in the woods during free time," said a boy with Einstein-like dark hair, "and these three guys from Camp Seneca came up and wanted us to move so they could trade baseball cards. But we didn't back down."

"That's great," Gabe said, wondering if one of the defeated had been Zack. He knew Zack had brought his baseball-card binder, and he knew Zack would find Element Cards to be incredibly nerdy, which was why Gabe had never mentioned them around him.

"Last week we probably would have left and gone to the library," a girl said, her cheeks turning the same shade of red as her three long braids. "But we stayed put, thanks to you."

"So we'd like to offer you one of our Element Cards," the dark-haired boy insisted, "to say thanks."

The red-haired girl held out a card that said "He," helium. "We figured one of the noble gases would be appropriate," she said with a shy smile.

"Noble gas!" said Three O'Clock with awe. He stared at the card, his forkful of Salisbury steak suspended near his mouth.

"Wow," Gabe said, his ears getting warm. "Are you sure? You guys were the ones who stood your ground."

"You gave us the idea," the girl with three braids insisted. "We never would have done it if you hadn't stood up to that guy on the playground. You're a hero."

"Well," Gabe said, torn. When they put it that way, he did deserve the card, and helium was hard to find. But a true hero should probably graciously turn down the reward. He was still mentally debating when Amanda Wisznewski appeared—out of nowhere, it seemed—and took the helium card. "Thank you," she said. "As Gabe's best friend and research partner, I accept this card on his behalf."

Gabe was too surprised to object. Amanda stood there and smiled until the younger kids, confused, headed awkwardly back to their own table. Amanda tucked the card in her shorts pocket, said, "You're welcome," and left.

Chapter 23

ZACK

That night, Camp Seneca gathered to watch *Man of Steel* on a big projection screen outside in the clearing. Afterward, as the end credits rolled and the Tomahawk boys were stretching and talking, Abbot ran in, crashing between Zack and RJ. His blond hair stuck to his pink forehead with sweat. At first Zack ignored him, but when they lined up to go to their bunks, Abbot's breathing was so fast and heavy—and right onto Zack's neck—that he couldn't take it anymore.

"Where were you?" Zack asked, glancing back.

"Who, me?" Abbot asked with a smirk. "I was sitting with you and RJ through the whole movie."

"Yeah, right," RJ said. "You left halfway. You missed all the best parts."

"Nope," said Abbot. "I was there the whole time. You guys can vouch for me. I was definitely *not* raiding the geeks' bunks."

Zack and RJ's eyes met over Abbot's sweaty back.

"Raiding their bunks?" Zack said. "What did you do?"

"I didn't do anything. Neither did Leo or Maddie."

Leo was another Tomahawk—a thick, mooselike guy who wore rugby shirts and took every game a little too seriously. Zack saw him at the front of the line; the back of his T-shirt was wet. There were a few Maddies, but Zack figured the one Abbot was referring to was the skinny blond one with big sunglasses and a biting laugh.

Marco came closer to their part of the line, so Zack kept quiet until they were back in the cabin. "Okay, *what* did you do?" Zack whispered as he unzipped his hoodie.

"For the last time," Abbot said, his sweaty shirt off and draped over his shoulder like a towel after a tough workout, "I didn't do anything. But the rumor is that *someone*"—he lowered his voice and stared into Zack's eyes, then RJ's, making clear that *someone* was him—"broke into the nerd huts, took

all the science cards, and hid them somewhere in the woods."
He smirked.

"You broke in?" RJ said loudly. Abbot and Zack gave him
a warning look, and he lowered his voice. "Dude, you're in so
much trouble."

Abbot took off his shorts and pulled on a pair of pajama
pants. "You're right. Breaking in sounds like something a
criminal would do. It's not like there are locks on cabin doors,
or like we had to go in through a window or something. So we
didn't break in to anything. *Snuck in* is a better term. We just
went in when no one was there." He sat on his bottom bed
and leaned against the wall with his hands behind his head,
as though reclining on a beach chair.

"But you stole their science cards," Zack said.

"Zack," Abbot said. He sat up and smiled at him as
though he were talking to a silly child. "I keep forgetting this
is your first summer at camp. Sneaking into bunks and stealing stuff isn't a crime here—it's a tradition! Last summer all
of Mohawk snuck into the girls' cabin, stole their bras, and
hung them around the skate park like streamers. It was hilarious. And then, for revenge, the girls snuck into the changing
room while we were showering and took all our dry clothes.

We had to walk back to our cabin in just towels, and they'd replaced our bath towels with these really small towels, like the kind you use for your hands!"

Zack looked at RJ and tried not to laugh, even though he was picturing Abbot sprinting from the shower building to his cabin with nothing but a dainty handtowel. That *was* funny. But it still seemed a little different to be sneaking into the SCGE bunks and taking all the Element Cards. "I don't know, dude," Zack said. "If it's such a tradition, why are you pretending you had nothing to do with it?"

Abbot didn't really have an answer for that. He just shrugged, picked up his toothbrush and toothpaste, and started out. He paused by the cabin door, then came back and grabbed his big bath towel too.

Chapter 24

GABE

During homework time, Gabe aggregated the data from his experiment. He reshaded the camp map to represent the land Summer Center had reclaimed. He estimated the number of Summer Center campers he'd seen outside during free time. And he recorded the account the kids had given him at lunch about the Element Cards. So far, the data pointed to a unanimous conclusion that proved his theory. He wrote: *Evidence suggests that Summer Center is becoming fun again.*

He thought: *All thanks to me!*

He sat up straight and looked around at all the kids whose lives he'd helped improve. Then he spent the rest of homework time drafting his original short story for Heroes. It was about a boy named Greg who wore thick glasses. In chapter one, an evil gang called the Skinters broke his glasses, and the shards went into Greg's eyes, making him blind. But within a few days, Greg's other senses compensated by getting stronger—so much stronger that he could smell danger and taste hidden toxins and hear people's thoughts. His name became Captain Sense-sation, and he was going to defeat the Skinters once and for all.

Gabe was so wrapped up in the story—Captain Sense-sation's sense of touch was so powerful, he could determine the inorganic makeup of a solid object simply by placing his pinky finger on it—that he completely missed the ice-cream sandwiches that were passed around for snack. "You can have mine," a girl from his research methods class said, holding it out. The half-melted ice cream was dripping through a seam in the paper wrapper. "Thanks for helping make camp fun again," she said.

"You're welcome," Gabe said gallantly. He enjoyed the sandwich, even though the chocolate adhered to his fingers and the ice cream oozed out the sides of the sticky cookies with each large, proud bite.

For his nighttime activity, making dream catchers, he instead used the leather, feathers, and beads to make himself a headdress, like the kind Crazy Horse might have worn when he defeated General Custer at Little Bighorn. He marched back to his bunk at nine, wearing his headdress and imagining himself a brave warrior returning triumphantly to his soldiers.

But something was off. His soldiers weren't in good spirits. Everyone was talking hysterically, swarming their counselors, and running around like ants whose hill had been stepped on.

Gabe spotted the girl with three braids who'd called him a hero at dinner. She was sitting on the steps outside her cabin, her head in her hands. "What's going on?" Gabe asked.

"We've been robbed!" she cried, looking up at him with fiery eyes. "Our cabin's a total mess. Our stuff is all over the place. And our Element Cards are gone—every last one of them."

Chapter 25

ZACK

Shortly after lights-out, when Zack was drifting into that hazy state on the way to sleep, Marco shouted for everyone to get up and come outside. In case there was anyone trying to stay in bed, he bleeped his bullhorn until every last Tomahawk had filed through the cabin and out the door.

Zack rubbed his eyes and took a place in the clump of boys. Squinting into the dark, he could see groups of groggy, pajama-clad campers in similar clumps outside the cabins on either side of his.

"Listen up!" Marco shouted. He didn't need the bullhorn. "It has come to our attention that someone broke into the

Summer Center cabins tonight, trashed their belongings, and stole certain items. This is absolutely unacceptable."

Zack tried to look at Abbot without moving his head or eyes. He couldn't see much, but he didn't sense any nervousness.

"We know that sharing this campground hasn't been ideal," Marco continued. "There's been some teasing, from both sides, and some arguments over who can use what space. But this is taking it to a new level. It's beyond disrespectful. I'm ashamed to think that anyone who goes to Camp Seneca—and especially anyone in the great Tomahawk bunk—would have something to do with this."

Zack's eyes had adjusted to the dark now, and he could see that Marco wasn't messing around. His lips were a forceful line, and his eyes were like lasers as they scanned the group. Zack kept staring straight ahead, trying to betray nothing but sleepiness. He hoped the Summer Center kids hadn't told anyone about their encounter in the woods during free time. If the smart people who ran Summer Center were anything like Gabe—which they had to be, except even smarter—and they knew that he and RJ and Abbot had argued with SCGE kids that very afternoon over using the table for trading Element Cards, they were sure to target them as suspects.

The Camp Seneca director walked up behind Marco. He, too, looked majorly peeved. "Tomahawk," the director said, "I'm sure Marco told you why we got you up. This is totally uncool. It is not the Seneca way. So here's the deal. Tomorrow, instead of your usual bunk activities, everyone in all of Camp Seneca will pitch in to clean the areas of our campground that SCGE has been so kind as to share with us. You boys were scheduled to"—he shined a flashlight at a clipboard—"go waterskiing." He smiled and raised his eyebrows. "Bummer. Instead of waterskiing, you'll be scrubbing the bathrooms, or maybe the cafeteria."

The campers began to protest, and the director turned his flashlight onto them until they stopped. "That's not all!" he shouted. "I want the items that were stolen back by twelve p.m. sharp. There will be a box in the camp office for them to be returned anonymously. Returning the stolen items is your get-out-of-jail-free pass. If they are not in that box by noon, we will figure out who took them, and they will be punished severely. I repeat: We will figure it out. You will not get away with this. And until we figure it out— no matter how long it takes—the whole camp will continue to pay. Is that clear?"

The boys mumbled and nodded.

The director nodded to Marco before moving on to deliver his speech to the next cabin.

Everyone shuffled back into the bunk. Most of them were grumbling about missing waterskiing and asking one another what had even happened. Zack, RJ, and Abbot were quiet, and Zack noticed that Leo, whose bed was in a different section of the cabin, was silent too.

Abbot flung himself onto his mattress, and Zack and RJ looked at each other from their top beds.

"Is cleaning the bathroom a camp tradition too?" Zack asked into the silence.

"Shut up," Abbot shot back.

They were all quiet for a whole minute. Then RJ said, "What are you going to do?"

Abbot sighed. Clearly he'd been thinking about it. "We're going to wait until everyone falls asleep, and then we're going to go get the cards and put them in that stupid box."

Zack realized Abbot's plan was the best course of action. If he waited until the morning, it'd be impossible to retrieve and return the cards without getting caught, and he didn't believe that that box was a total get-out-of-jail-free pass, not if the director saw who filled it. "Where are they?" Zack asked.

"By the lake," Abbot said. "In this hole near the kayaking stuff. Can you guys come help?"

"No way," RJ said. "I'm not getting in trouble."

"Come on, man," Abbot whined. "It's too much stuff for me and Leo to carry ourselves in one trip, and there's no way we can get Maddie from her bunk without getting caught."

You should've thought of that when you stole it all, Zack thought angrily. What did he care if Abbot got caught? It was bad enough that the whole camp was already being punished for his "tradition."

On the other hand, they still had four weeks left of camp, and he had to live in the bed above Abbot for all of them. Life was going to be seriously unpleasant if Abbot got caught but not kicked out. And who's to say Abbot wouldn't take him and RJ down with him? They'd been in the woods with the Element Cards that day, and if Abbot claimed they'd helped him steal the cards, it'd be their word against his.

Zack rolled over and punched his pillow at the injustice of it. A sinking feeling in his stomach made him realize that even though he had nothing to do with the raid, he still felt somewhat responsible for it. Like his people had let

Gabe down. He wanted to be able to tell his brother that he'd helped make it right.

"I'll help," he said firmly. "But if we get caught, you have to *swear* you'll tell the director I had nothing to do with the raid. And either way, you'll owe me *big time*."

"Yeah, yeah, I swear," Abbot said. "Thanks, Zack. I knew you were cool."

"Are you crazy?" RJ whispered from his top bed to Zack's.

"Probably," Zack admitted. He rolled to the side of the mattress and looked down at Abbot. "Kick my bed when you want to leave."

Zack had finally fallen into a blissful sleep when he felt a hand shaking him awake. "Come on," Abbot whispered.

Zack yawned, rubbed his eyes, and peered over the edge of his bed. Abbot was standing there, as was Leo. Zack held his wrist to the moonlight coming in through the window. 1:22 a.m. He considered rolling over and letting them go without him, but instead peeled off his sleeping bag and climbed quietly down the ladder. He pulled on his sweatshirt, slid his feet into his sandals, and stuck his flashlight in the pocket of the hoodie. "Okay," he whispered back. "Let's get this over with."

They tiptoed through the cabin, past Marco's room, and, with a frighteningly loud squeak of the cabin door, into the cold, damp night. They stayed silent while Abbot and Leo led the way into the woods, turning their flashlights on only once they were deep enough in for the beams to disappear into the trees. Zack remembered last summer, when he'd gotten a letter from Gabe about kayaking to Dead Man's Island by himself in the middle of the night. The eeriness of the woods at this hour—the way every crack of a twig or skitter of a leaf made goose bumps rise on Zack's skin—gave him newfound respect for his stepbrother. It also gave him some added respect for himself. Sure, the circumstances weren't great, but this would make a pretty awesome story.

They reached the lake undetected, and then stepped carefully down the path to the shed that housed the kayaking equipment. Zack shined his light into Abbot's eyes. "Where are the cards?" he whispered.

Abbot batted Zack's flashlight away and pointed his own to the side of the shed. Leo followed the beam, walking slowly and shining his light on the ground until it revealed a pit with patches of color peeking through loose dirt. Zack shook his head and rolled his eyes. At least they hadn't buried the cards more thoroughly; this would make it easier to dig them up.

As they threw the dirt aside and unearthed the stash, Zack started to wonder how they'd gotten all these cards here in the first place. It was a huge pit, and it was completely full of Element Cards, some in binders, some in rubber-banded stacks, and others loose. Abbot had been right that it was too much for him and Leo to carry on their own. They would have needed all of Tomahawk to get these cards to the camp office in one trip.

"How'd you guys get all these here?" Zack asked.

"Maddie's suitcase," Abbot said.

Zack couldn't help but be impressed. These three people had managed to sneak away during a movie, break into SCGE's bunks, find the Element Cards, and transport them across the field and through the woods *in a suitcase* without being detected. If it weren't so mean and didn't get the whole camp punished, it would be pretty hilarious.

"Well, how are we going to bring them back?" Zack asked. "It's too much to carry."

"I can carry a lot," Leo said. He stooped down and loaded his arms with two binders, a few stacks, and a mess of loose cards. As he stood up, the loose cards dropped, and the stacks followed. Leo stared at them dumbly.

"We could take a few trips," Abbot said. But they all knew this was a bad idea. They were lucky to have made it this far without getting caught. Going back and forth was just asking for trouble.

What would Gabe do? Zack thought. *He always figures out smart solutions to this kind of thing.* He looked around, trying to see the situation with Gabe's eyes, bifocals and all. It worked. "I've got it," Zack said. Abbot and Leo followed him back around the shed to the row of kayaks resting on the ground. He shined his flashlight at the kayaks and grinned.

The three of them were walking across the dark field carrying a kayak filled with dirty binders and science trading cards when they heard footsteps. And whistling. Zack's legs froze but his heart went into overdrive. The three of them were rooted to the spot, their arms aching from the weight of the kayak, and Zack couldn't do anything but close his eyes.

"Zack?" said a voice.

Zack opened his eyes. It was Zig. He must have been just coming back from working at the restaurant. "Hey, Zig," Zack said weakly.

Cicadas hummed.

Zig took in the scene, his lips curling up at one edge. "Take it easy, Zack," he said finally. "See you in the kitchen tomorrow."

Back in his bed, with the loaded kayak safely outside the camp office, Zack stared up at the ceiling and smiled. Summer camp was pretty cool.

Chapter 26
GABE

Gabe didn't know what the opposite of a hero was—not really a villain, he hoped, more like a dud—but whatever it was, that's how he felt. When he woke up the next morning and saw his headdress hanging limply from his bedpost, he remembered the events from last night, and the pit of his stomach knotted.

In the bed across from Gabe, Wesley stretched his legs and wrangled his arms out of his twisted sleeping bag. "I had a dream that I was in Periodic Table Land," he said, "and all of the elements had been kidnapped. The ransom note said they'd be returned in exchange for six Snickers bars."

"That's all?" Gabe said.

Wesley rolled onto his side and scratched his head. "You're right. That doesn't seem like a lot now. In my dream it was unthinkable."

That explained Gabe's vague recollection of Wesley shouting "Unthinkable!" in the middle of the night. "I'd trade six *hundred* Snickers bars to get the cards back," Gabe said now, "since it's my fault they're gone."

"Don't feel bad," said Nikhil, who was already up and folding his sleeping bag. "It's not your fault the Camp Seneca kids are criminals."

Gabe sighed. "Amanda said there's no point in fighting if you're going to lose. Maybe she's right. My idea only made everything worse."

"I don't know," Nikhil said. "You didn't really expect Camp Seneca to back down so easily, right? To just concede the territories back to us? I mean, I didn't expect them to plunder and pillage, but I did expect them to do *something*."

"Yeah," Wesley agreed. "The war's just getting started. You should wear your headdress to breakfast."

"No way," Gabe said. "I feel stupid for even making it. If I wasn't so proud of myself, maybe it wouldn't have happened."

"Hubris," said Three O'Clock.

Nikhil nodded. "That was one of my spelling bee words. It means extreme pride."

"Oh yeah!" Wesley said. He started trying to get out of his sleeping bag. "Hubris is what causes a lot of heroes of Greek tragedies to fail in the end." He wiggled until the sleeping bag dropped over the edge of the bed and landed at Nikhil's feet. Nikhil picked it up, folded it, and handed it back.

"Thanks." Wesley climbed down the ladder. "Since you think the headdress caused you tragic hubris, Gabe, can I wear it?"

Gabe shrugged. "If you want."

Wesley wore the headdress all through breakfast, even though the beads kept dipping into his cereal as he ate. He finally had to take it off when the camp director stood in front of the cafeteria with an important announcement and the table behind Gabe's complained that the feathers were blocking their view.

"Good morning!" the director said. "I'm sure you're all ready for a new day after the events of last night."

The collective grumbling suggested that no one was excited about a new day.

"I have some great news," the director continued. "The stolen Element Cards have been returned. The Camp Seneca director found them outside the gymnasium this morning. The bad news is that they were in a kayak, so they're a bit wet and dirty. Also, apart from the ones that were in binders labeled with names, it's going to be difficult to match cards with their original owners." The director kept talking over the rising chatter. "All the cards will be in the camp office, and your counselors will be bringing you over in shifts to try to match cards with owners."

The girl who'd given Gabe the helium card raised her hand. "Did they catch the person who stole them?"

"And kick them out of camp?" another girl asked.

"Yeah!" a boy shouted.

"Off with their heads!" someone else called.

Everyone started talking at once, and the camp director had to blow her whistle to restore order. "That is none of your concern," she said sternly. "It is up to the Camp Seneca director to determine an appropriate punishment, and believe me, he is not treating this lightly. But you are Summer Center students, and I expect better from you than chanting 'off with their heads.' You're here to expand your minds, to grow as learners and citizens. I know that not everyone is happy to be sharing the campground, but you know what? We have four more weeks of camp. The Camp Seneca director and I are going to come up with some ways to build respect and camaraderie.

With all the brainpower in this room, I'm sure you can understand that this summer will be what you make of it."

Gabe didn't know whether to be inspired or deflated by the director's speech. He felt kind of like the returned Element Cards: intact but soggy. Even if what the director said was true, he was nervous to think himself capable of making a difference again. Look what had happened the first time he'd let himself get taken over by hubris. *Captain Sense-sation,* he thought. He should probably tear up that story and throw it in the trash.

Passing the Camp Seneca kids on the way out of the cafeteria was worse than it had ever been. They all mumbled apologies as they filed by, clearly having been instructed to by their counselors, but their faces were universally sour. *Why are* you *so annoyed?* Gabe thought. *We're the ones whose stuff was raided and stolen.*

In Research Methods, he glumly updated his research findings:

Problem: What will make SCGE fun again?
Hypothesis: SCGE will be fun if we don't let the
 Seneca kids run the campground.

Experiment: Stop hiding in our bunks. Stand up to Camp
   Seneca!
Results: Good for a few days, then Camp Seneca
   retaliated.

His teacher had said that sometimes an experiment could fail, but the hypothesis might still be accurate. This had to be one of those times. They'd already tried sulking around and letting the Camp Seneca kids bring them down; that certainly hadn't made camp fun. Standing their ground during free time didn't seem to work either. That didn't mean he should give up—it meant he should develop a new experiment.

He tried to summon the attitude he'd had in Mr. Justice's class: It's okay if you fail, as long as you try. That was certainly a lot easier to say than to experience. The truth was, Gabe realized with a strange awareness, that he wasn't used to failing at things. Failure was a new sensation for him, and it made his whole body weak, like his bones had turned into cooked spaghetti.

He looked around the room at his classmates hunched over their scientific journals. Most of these kids probably weren't used to failing either. No wonder they were all feeling so lousy.

* * *

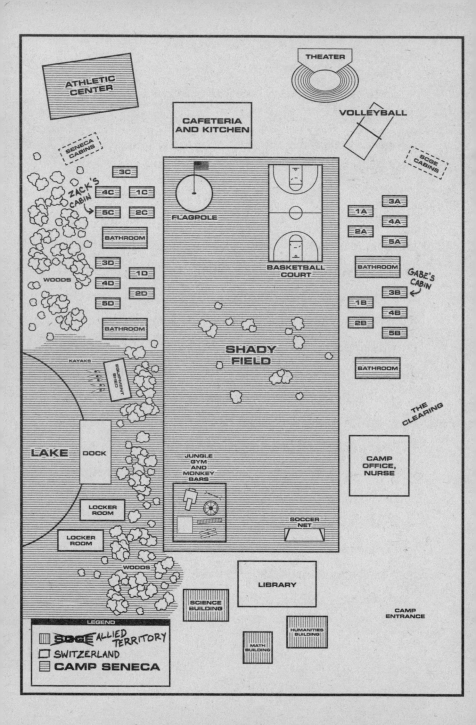

By recess, word had gotten around as to why the Camp Seneca kids were so annoyed: As a punishment for the raid, all of them had to spend their activity periods cleaning the campground. "*That's* why the bathrooms are so spic and span," Wesley said as he bumped a volleyball to Gabe. "I could see my reflection in the faucet."

"How'd you look?" Nikhil asked.

"Beautiful," said Wesley. He was still wearing the headdress.

"Why are they mad at *us*, though?" Gabe said, passing the ball to Three O'Clock. "They were getting in trouble for something one of their own did."

"We're talking about Camp Seneca here," Wesley said conspiratorially. "Intelligence isn't one of their strong suits. No offense to your brother."

My brother, Gabe thought, somewhat surprised. Zack wouldn't have had anything to do with the Element Cards, right?

Nikhil caught the ball and held it. "C^2 at your six o'clock, Gabe."

Three O'Clock said, "Six o'clock. Two-times-me!"

They all laughed, even though Gabe knew Nikhil meant that C^2 was coming up directly behind him. He stood straight and was prepared for the tap on his shoulder.

"Hey, Gabe," C^2 said. "Hey, guys. Did you hear why the Seneca kids are so pissed?"

"Yeah," Gabe said. "They had to clean the campground."

"Right. According to them, it was all a big joke we should've let slide. But you were right, man, we can't just let stuff like that slide."

"Right," Gabe said, wondering if he sounded sure of himself.

"Yeah!" said Wesley.

C^2 raised a fist in solidarity with Wesley, who grinned. Then he said to Gabe, "You have a brother who goes to Camp Seneca, right?"

"Stepbrother, yeah."

"So you have some insight into how the Camp Seneca mind works. What would your stepbrother say about this whole situation?"

Gabe tapped his nose, thinking. "He'd probably say we're asking for trouble by being so nerdy."

C^2 nodded, his eyes narrowing in thought. After a few seconds, he stopped nodding and put his hand firmly on Gabe's shoulder. "It's time for us to make our next move. Gather your best people, and let's meet in the clearing during free time to plan our attack."

Chapter 27

ZACK

Zack yawned for the fifth time in two minutes, and Lauren poked him with the handle of her scrub brush. Most of the Tomahawk boys, including Abbot and Leo, were cleaning the lower boys' bathroom, but Zig had requested that only experienced chefs (the campers who'd signed up for cooking for the third week in a row) clean the kitchen. Zack and Lauren were side by side, with matching yellow gloves and blue scrub brushes, trying to loosen flakes of burned food from the stove grates. Lauren had on a black tank top, her hair was pulled back in a messy bun, and the dimple in her cheek showed when she clenched her mouth in focus. Zack thought this punishment wasn't turning out to be so bad.

"Why are you so tired?" Lauren asked.

Zack began to work on a particularly charred area of the stove, wondering if the scrubbing motion made his arms look muscular. "It took me forever to fall asleep after that speech from the director last night," he said.

"Yeah, me too," Lauren said. "But I'm acting alive. You're like a zombie."

"What can I say? I need my beauty rest," Zack joked.

Lauren rolled her eyes and dipped her scrub brush in the sink, which was filled with soapy water. "So you're not tired because you had something to do with those cards getting mysteriously returned in the middle of the night?"

Zack focused on the stove. "Nope," he said. "Not me."

"What do you think about the cards being stolen?" Lauren asked.

Zack shrugged and kept his gaze on the stove. "It's kind of funny, but it's kind of mean. My stepbrother goes to Summer Center. He loves that kind of stuff."

Lauren stopped working and looked at Zack with surprise. "Your stepbrother goes to Summer Center, like, this summer? Here?"

"Yep."

"Is he really nerdy, like people say they are?"

"Yeah," Zack said with a laugh. "But he's kind of cool, too."

Lauren smiled and moved on to a new grate. They worked for a few minutes in silence before she said, "So, your stepbrother goes to Summer Center. Is that why you helped return the cards, even though you didn't steal them?"

Zack tried to hide his surprise, but he must not have done a very good job because Lauren started laughing. "How'd you know?" he asked her.

"Everyone knows. But I know from Maddie." Lauren crossed her arms and shook her head, but she was smiling. "I can't believe it."

"Can't believe what?"

"That you'd cover for her. Does your stepbrother know what you did?"

"No," Zack said. "I haven't even seen him since the first day of camp."

"Wait till he finds out," Lauren said. "He'll think you're a hero."

Did that mean she thought he was one? "Nah," Zack said. But he turned around to clean his brush, hoping Lauren wouldn't see that he was blushing.

Chapter 28

GABE

The Save Summer Center Squad (the "Sssquad") convened in the clearing at five p.m. sharp. Gabe was honored to be considered one of C^2's best people, especially given the results of his last stand. With him were his three bunkmates, plus the girl with three braids who'd given him the helium card, whose name, he found out, was Serafina. C^2 brought a bunkmate who barely talked but projected a cool aura of self-confidence. Jenny Chin was there, since she was C^2's sister, and that meant, of course, that Amanda was with her.

C^2 called the meeting to order, then reviewed the events

that had transpired between the two camps. Gabe had brought the camp map that showed the areas controlled by each army, and he and his bunkmates shared it with the Sssquad.

"I'll now open it up to the Sssquad," C² said. "Any ideas for how we can reclaim our camp?"

"We can get them back for stealing our cards," Serafina said. "Steal something of theirs, like their . . . sports cards or whatever it is they collect."

"But look at how much trouble they got in for it," Nikhil pointed out. "We don't want to upset the director, or our whole camp."

"We can get them back some other way," Wesley suggested. "Infest them with lice!"

"Let's not start *that* again," said Jenny, who'd gotten lice three times during last summer's infestation. C² agreed, and Nikhil was visibly relieved.

"We should show them we're cool," Amanda offered. "Not give them a reason to make fun of us."

Gabe knew from his time with Zack how stressful that was. "Summer Center is supposed to be where we can be ourselves," he said. "Remember how boring it was in the beginning, when we just let them do everything *they* wanted to do?"

Wesley blew air through his lips. "Who wants to be cool, anyway?"

"They're right," C^2 said. "Camp Seneca is threatening our society and our values. Trying to act like them means they win. We have to *defend* our way of life." As he got going, it became clear that he'd thought all this through before, and listening to the Sssquad's ideas had just been a formality. "There are a lot of us. What we need is a united front that asserts our right to our own camp."

"Yeah!" said Wesley. He put his hand firmly on Three O'Clock's shoulder, and Three gave a solid blink.

"Too much pride can be our downfall," Nikhil warned. "Hubris."

"No!" C^2 said, raising a pointer finger in the air. "What we need is *more* pride. They think their worst nightmare is being at Smart Camp for Geeks and Eggheads? Fine. Let's show them just how geeky we can be."

C^2's enthusiasm was getting Gabe's blood pumping, refueling his body and reinvigorating his mind. It was being in a group like this, brainstorming, that made camp feel like camp. Looking around at the group, everything finally felt right. Why shouldn't they be proud of that?

"I think you're on to something," Amanda said. "Gabe and I were talking about the Civil Rights Movement today." She smiled at Gabe, as though the two of them had been discussing the Civil Rights Movement over a private candlelit dinner rather than having learned about it in a classroom surrounded by other kids.

Something clicked in Gabe's brain. "Yes! When we used the campgrounds during free time, we were kind of like Rosa Parks, who refused to give up her seat on the bus. But we can step it up. We can do something proactive."

"I like where this is going," C² said. "We have to be as nerdy as possible, and show them we're proud of it."

Amanda jumped up. "A march!" she said. "Civil Rights activists marched on Washington."

Jenny clapped once. "We could march on Shady Field."

"A march . . ." said Nikhil. "You mean, like, a parade?"

"I like it," Gabe said. "A Nerd Pride parade."

"Can we dress like brains?" Serafina asked excitedly. "I'll be the frontal lobe."

"Oh man," said Wesley. "I was *just* about to call frontal lobe."

"Brains on Parade," said C², nodding in approval. Everyone

began talking excitedly, but C² called them back to attention. "Okay, let's plan the parade for Friday free time. That will give us a few days to get ready. We'll need signs, music, the works."

Gabe had a momentary flash of Zack watching him lead a Nerd Pride parade, and his palms began to sweat. Was this really the right decision? But C² was having everyone put their hands in for a parting chant. Gabe forced the thought of Zack away and threw his clammy hand into the pile.

"All right, Sssquad," C² said. "We're nerdy, we're proud, and we're *here*. Camp Seneca isn't going to know what hit them."

Chapter 29

ZACK

Gabe's dinosaur underwear stared at Zack every time he opened his drawer, and every morning he'd vow that this would be the day he'd return it. But with bunk activities and nighttime campfires and cooking well into free time, he found himself looking at the underwear again every night, another day having passed without seeing Gabe.

On Friday, the cooking group met early for a field trip to Zig's restaurant, an experience Zig promised would "blow their culinary minds." Zack wasn't disappointed. They were met at the restaurant by the head chef, a woman named Linda who was friendly but also strict with her cooks. It was clear that she was Zig's boss, which was as strange to Zack as the time his mom made him go clothes shopping and his history teacher from school was the one working the register. But it was also reassuring to see that even someone as cool and confident as Zig was still learning the ropes.

Chef Linda gave them a tour of the kitchen, which was big and hot and filled with sounds of chopping and blending and searing. Zig pointed out equipment and techniques they had or used back at camp, but he also showed them things that were totally different and unexpected. "Chef Linda likes to take risks with her food," Zig said. "For instance, in this container, this one with a warning, we have ghost chili peppers, some of the hottest chilies in the world."

"I ate a jalapeño once on a dare," Zack said. "I thought my mouth was going to explode."

"I bet," Zig said. "But get this." He put on a pair of plastic gloves, opened the container, and took out one of the peppers. "The heat of a pepper is measured in something called Scoville heat units. The higher the rating, the hotter the pepper. A jalapeño is rated at about three thousand units. Guess how much the ghost chili is?"

"Five thousand?" Lauren guessed.

"Ten thousand?" Zack tried.

Zig smirked. "About one million units."

Every jaw dropped. Zack wasn't great at math, but Chef Linda was. "That's more than three hundred times hotter than that jalapeño you ate," she said.

"And you cook with them?" Zack asked, incredulous.

Chef Linda laughed. "We use just a tiny bit to flavor a large amount of food. You have to be careful when you handle them too—that's why Zig is wearing gloves. If you touch a ghost pepper and then you touch your eye, it could burn your eye."

Zack stared at the pepper Zig was holding and imagined the danger. Wait till he told RJ and Abbot about ghost chilies. "Cooking is so freaking cool," he said.

Chef Linda beamed. "It sure is," she said. "Why don't you take that pepper back with you, Zig? You can put it up on a high shelf, but it'll remind your chefs in training how cool cooking can be."

Zig said that was a great idea. He put the pepper in a plastic bag and used a marker to write *DANGER: DO NOT HANDLE* on the outside.

"Let me show you some other cool things about cooking,"

Chef Linda said. "Have any of you heard of molecular gastronomy?"

Molecular gastronomy, Zack learned, was this experimental way of cooking that made food into weird textures, like foams and spheres and gels. One of the other chefs put on goggles and gloves and demonstrated making something using liquid nitrogen, which made Zack feel like he was at a science museum rather than a restaurant. *I have to tell Gabe about this*, he thought. *When I get back to camp, I'm going to find him, return his underwear, and tell him about molecular gastronomy, no matter what.*

The bus got them back to camp right before free time, and Zack was still fired up. He raced to his bunk, grabbed the dinosaur underwear, and set out in search of his stepbrother.

But there didn't seem to be any SCGE kids around. They weren't on the field or in the playground. Zack jogged through the woods (only Seneca kids), by the academic buildings (empty), and down by the lake (nope). He was going to go over to the SCGE bunks when he heard some noise coming from the far end of the field. He stayed still, straining to listen. It sounded like a fistfight, or cheerleading practice, or a marching band getting in tune—or all three. And it was getting closer.

Other kids were hearing it too. A soccer game came to a halt, a frisbee sailed into the distance without being caught, and hand games stopped midclap. RJ came up behind Zack. "What's going on?"

"No clue," Zack said. "But whatever it is, it's coming toward us." He pointed to the far side of the field, where a giant mass of . . . *something* was moving. Getting bigger.

Seneca kids came out of the woods and off the play-ground, lining up along the sides of the field to see what was going to happen. The anticipation was building; Zack's heart was pumping like he was at a rock concert waiting for the band to come onstage.

Abbot found Zack and RJ. He pushed himself between them and wrapped one arm around each of their shoulders. "Duuuude," he said. "This must be the annual parade in my honor."

Zack pushed Abbot's arm away and stood on his tiptoes. The pack was getting closer. "It does look like a parade," he said.

The music started to get louder, but it didn't sound like typical parade music. It didn't sound like rock music either. As they got closer, Zack's forehead wrinkled. It was . . . classical music? A mini orchestra of kids, with violins, clarinets, a tuba, an oboe, and two French horns. They stopped right by Zack and played a minuet or a concerto or something. Zack and RJ looked at each other, but neither had an explanation.

When the musicians finished, the parade began in earnest with a group of kids carrying a banner that said SCGE PRESENTS: BRAINS ON PARADE! Behind them marched kids wearing lab coats and carrying steaming test tubes in metal clamps. Three boys waddled past in big boxes painted to look like calculators. Some girls danced by, twirling batons. One threw hers up in the air and it landed on another girl, giving her a bloody nose. She had to step to the side of the parade and pull some tissues from her fanny pack. There were other musicians scattered throughout, and lots of big, carefully lettered signs that said things like NERD PRIDE! PRESERVE THE SANCTITY OF SMART CAMP! THE GEEK SHALL INHERIT THE EARTH!

Zack and the other spectators were rooted in place, shocked silent, their mouths hanging open in disbelief.

The whole parade stopped and began to sing to the tune of "Yankee Doodle":

"A bunch of smart kids went to camp
Brighter than the sun

Camp Seneca made fun of them
But could not spoil their fun!

Geeks and eggheads, keep it up
Be brainy boys and girls
Dumb Senecas cannot stop us
We nerds will rule the world!"

Abbot moaned in horror.

RJ whispered, "What. The. Heck."

Zack winced. *Maybe Gabe isn't a part of this,* Zack thought hopefully. Realizing he was holding the package of dinosaur underwear, he quickly stuffed it into the back of his shorts and covered it with his shirt. What were these loonies *thinking*?

There was one event left, and it must have been their attempt at a grand finale: a giant, lumpy brain made out of papier-mâché, with a few kids pushing it and others riding it like a float. Zack squeezed his eyes as it approached. He peeked out nervously as it passed. On top of the brain were a few kids waving like Santa Claus at the end of the Macy's Thanksgiving Day parade. These kids must have been the leaders behind this.

Oh no, Zack thought. He closed his eyes again. Abbot poked him in the ribs until he opened them, then turned his finger to the kings of the giant brain, one of whom was wearing a night brace with baseball cards tucked under the strap. "That's Zack's brother!" Abbot shouted.

Zack let down his shoulders and shook his head. He'd found Gabe.

Chapter 30

GABE

When the Sssquad arrived outside the cafeteria, wrapping up the parade, they were greeted with shouts and cheers and pats on the back. Gabe climbed down from the top of the brain, his heart pumping.

"Did you see their *faces*?" said a boy dressed as a graphing calculator.

"Priceless," said a girl as she practiced some scales on her violin.

"That was *so* cool," said a baton twirler, her head tipped back with a tissue stuffed in her nose.

"Awesome squared," agreed another calculator. He punched some numbers on his costume and then made a show of hitting the squared button.

C^2 tapped on the side of the brain with a ruler and pushed his big chemistry goggles up onto his head. "Attention, everyone." The crowd got quiet and turned toward him, a sea of grinning faces in a suspended bubble of revelry. "Great job. Way to show our nerd pride."

Everyone whooped and jumped. Gabe high-fived Three O'Clock. Amanda gave him a hug, and he didn't think twice about hugging her back.

"The key thing now," C^2 continued, "is that we keep it up. Do the nerdiest things you can, and don't back down, no matter how Camp Seneca reacts. This is our place, and it's our time. Let's use our brains!"

A collective cheer gave way, organically, to the whole camp singing the nerd pride anthem. Those with instruments joined in, building in volume and intensity as the song progressed.

Gabe was trying to keep his hubris in check, to not consider any of his deeds heroic until the scientific method proved them so, and the results of this experiment had yet to be seen. But wearing his night brace, surrounded by his camp friends, standing next to a papier-mâché brain, it was hard not to believe it was true as they belted out the last line: *"We nerds will rule the world!"*

Gabe and his bunkmates got to keep part of the giant brain—the cerebellum—in their room. It doubled as a nightstand for Nikhil and Three O'Clock, whose beds were on the bottom, and a stepping stone for Wesley and Gabe to reach theirs on top. It was also a good stepstool for hanging up additional decorations; the counselors were hosting a bunk-decorating competition as a nighttime activity, and it was generally understood that the nerdiest decorations would win. They were putting up a banner with pi to the fortieth digit, a poster that had an entire Shakespeare play written in a tiny font, one of the NERDS RULE posters from the parade, and printed-out images of famous teams: the three musketeers; peanut butter and jelly; and sine, cosine, and tangent.

The three days that had passed since the parade were like Summer Center magnified by a million percent. The Summer Center campers walked around wearing their head gear, lab coats, fanny packs, and pocket protectors. Kids with contacts put their glasses on instead, and those who didn't need glasses made fake ones out of pencils and pipe cleaners. Nikhil's surgical masks were in high demand, and he was happy to lend out all but a small reserve stash, in case of a real emergency. Free time turned into Nerd Pride time. The jungle gym became a physics test ground, the lake a marine biology laboratory, and the woods a historical reenactment theater.

The Senecas mocked them, but the Summer Center campers stood united. They didn't fix their Seneca-given wedgies, but instead toddled around with them proudly, brandishing them like war injuries. A young Summer Center kid got made fun of for reading in the clearing, and the next day, his whole bunk spread their swim towels across the basketball court, lay down on them, and read. The Senecas, furious, stomped back to their bunks, which was one of the only territories on the map still in their jurisdiction.

The Summer Center director began giving speeches at almost every meal, encouraging the campers, with increasing exasperation, to be open-minded and share their campground. "You're welcome to read during free time," she said at breakfast on Monday, "but you don't have to do it on the basketball court. Let that be for people who want to play basketball."

Serafina raised her hand. "Why would anyone want to play basketball?" she said with a derisive snort. "You don't learn anything doing it."

People clapped and agreed, even though Gabe figured most of them would also agree with Nikhil, who whispered that it does require strategy. "You could also use math to figure out the ideal shot trajectory," he said, mostly to his cup of yogurt.

Gabe didn't mention that basketball could also just be fun, and that last summer it was a popular choice for free time and nighttime activities. The same was true of kayaking, which had become off-limits unless you were going to experiment with paddle stroke techniques to test drag; and also doing cannonballs off the dock into the lake, which was something only "stupid Senecas" did. Sports and cannonballs were small sacrifices in the name of Nerd Pride, and for a few gloriously geeky days, SCGE was in control of the campground.

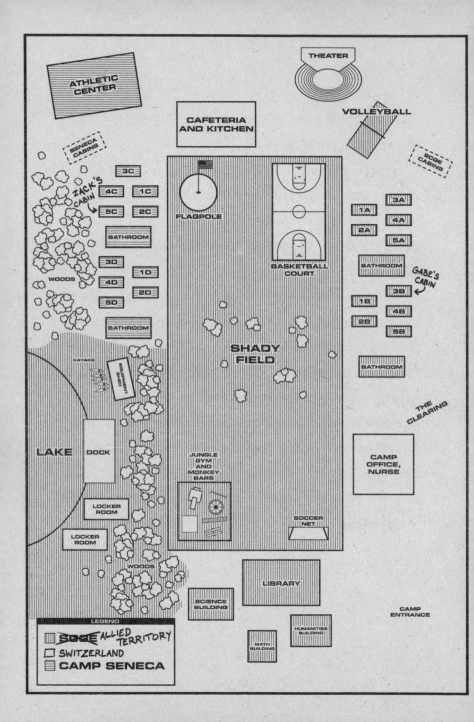

Chapter 31

ZACK

Things were heating up at Camp Seneca. The weather was unusually steamy, which made everyone sweaty and cranky. With the avalanche of in-your-face geekiness, things were ready to boil over.

On Tuesday afternoon, the air conditioning in the kitchen failed while Zack was cooking. A bead of sweat dripped from his forehead onto the stove. "I don't think that's what Zig meant when he said to sweat the onions," Lauren joked.

"Ha-ha," Zack said weakly. He wiped his hairline with his forearm.

"Sorry," Lauren said. "The heat is turning me into a bad comedian."

Zig held a meat thermometer in the air. "Ninety-three," he read. "Yowza. Let's call it quits for today."

Zack peeled off his apron and used it to dry his neck. He left without saying good-bye to anyone; he needed to change into board shorts and cannonball into the lake. When he got to the cabin, RJ was there, already in his swimsuit.

"Did you guys lose AC too?" RJ asked. "I was playing Uno in the gym, and it got so hot, the cards were sticking together."

"Try losing AC when you're sautéing onions," Zack said. "It was almost a hundred degrees in the kitchen." He pulled a pair of board shorts out of his drawer, and the package of Gabe's dinosaur underwear fell to the floor. Zack let it lie. He didn't have time to think about anything but the cold lake.

"Let's go," RJ said when Zack had changed.

Outside, the sun burned down through the moist air. "It's too hot to run," Zack moaned, "but I want to get there faster."

"Let's jog," RJ said. "Remember how freezing the water was the first day of camp? I hope it's even colder now. I'd trade a 1952 Mickey Mantle card for an ice bath right now."

"Would you really?" Zack asked. A rookie Mickey Mantle card would be worth over $200,000.

"I don't know," RJ said. "It's too hot for deep questions. The sun is melting my brain."

When they reached the lake, they dropped their shoulders instead of their towels. It was only four thirty, which meant some Summer Center campers were still there for their swim time. They were splashing and laughing, and Zack's sweaty fingers itched to join them.

"I'm sorry," one of the lifeguards said, "but they're not done until 4:45. I can't let you in if you're not part of these bunks."

"Please?" Zack asked. "We got out of our activities early because the air conditioning broke. Can't we just cool off?"

"We won't stay long," RJ promised. "We'll just jump in and out."

The lifeguard frowned and swung her whistle around her finger. "I can't let you in now. But if you come back in fifteen minutes, I'll let you dunk before free time begins."

Zack sighed. Fifteen minutes might as well have been an eternity. "All right."

"In the meantime," the lifeguard said, "you should go

into the library. It's always air conditioned because of the computers in there."

Zack and RJ set off in the direction the lifeguard had pointed. Lauren caught up with them on the way.

"Hey!" she said, catching her breath. "You guys look like you're on a mission. Do you have a secret trick to cool off?"

"As a matter of fact," Zack said, "we do. Get ready to be amazed."

"Ooh," Lauren said with a smile.

They reached the library building, and sure enough, it must have been cold in there. Through the front windows, they could see Summer Center campers inside, talking in a group and holding books. One of the campers opened the door to leave, and a gust of icy air escaped. Zack, RJ, and Lauren gave a collective "Aaah."

Zack reached out to hold the door, but the exiting camper caught it and stood in his way. "Do you go to Camp Seneca?" she asked.

"Yes," Zack said.

The girl stood up straight. She opened the door and stuck her head inside. "Intruders!" she announced. "Seneca intruders! Assume your posts!"

RJ and Lauren looked at each other. Zack stayed by the door, enjoying the cold breeze that was leaking through.

The girl came back, this time flanked by two other Summer Center campers. One was extremely tall and lanky, and his white lab coat covered his shorts, making it look like he wasn't wearing any clothes at all. The other was short and stocky with lensless glasses that looked like they were made from a bent clothes hanger and pieces of masking tape. The three of them stood in a line in front of the now-closed door, blocking the entrance like the world's goofiest security guards.

"This is a Summer Center building," Lab Coat said. "State the purpose of your mission."

"Uh," Zack said. He glanced back at his friends. "We're here to cool off. We're really hot, and the AC died on our part of the campground."

Fake Glasses smirked. "Libraries are for feeding your brain, not for cooling off. Access denied."

"Come on," RJ said, rolling his eyes and letting his head drop back. "Can't we just step inside for one second?"

"What makes you think you're deserving of entering Geekland?" Lab Coat asked.

Lauren crossed her arms. "What makes you think we're not?"

"I know!" the girl in the center said. "How about they can come in if they prove themselves worthy"—she looked at her fellow guards—"by solving the riddle of the Sphinx."

"The riddle of the Sphinx?" Zack repeated.

The kids guffawed—not just laughed, but actually guffawed—and Zack felt a bead of sweat drip from his back.

"He doesn't even know what the riddle of the Sphinx is!" Fake Glasses said.

"That doesn't mean he can't solve it," Lauren said. "Right, Zack?"

Zack swallowed. He was pretty sure it did mean he couldn't solve it. Now he'd have to prove Lauren wrong, and these weirdoes right, and be humiliated in front of everyone.

"You have one chance to answer this riddle," the center guard pronounced. She cleared her throat. "What has one voice and yet becomes four-footed and two-footed and three-footed?"

Zack's insides turned to mush. *What?* he thought. Weren't riddles supposed to be funny? He didn't even know what he was being asked. Something about a voice and feet and math? Did Gabe know this stuff? Probably, but he wouldn't use it to make other people feel like idiots.

"Well," Lab Coat said. "Have you come up with an answer? The air inside is a frosty sixty-five degrees."

Guess something, Zack told himself. It could be anything. *A song? Some kind of animal? A yardstick?* They said this was the riddle of the Sphinx. Wasn't the Sphinx in Europe or something? Did the answer have to do with traveling? His palms might as well have been coated with Crisco.

"You have five seconds to answer," the center guard declared.

Say something, Zack thought.

"Four, three, two . . ."

Take a guess!

"One!" the three nerds shouted. Fake Glasses made a buzzer noise.

The girl in the center shook her head. "It's official: You can't enter. No low-IQs allowed."

Now Zack's whole body was hot, like a pot of water coming to a simmer. "Why do you guys have to be so *weird*?" he spat. "That was the stupidest riddle I ever heard."

Lab Coat smiled pityingly. "I think we proved which one of us is stupid," he said, and the other two guffawed again.

"Whatever," Lauren said. She put her hand on Zack's shoulder. "Come on."

"Yeah," said RJ. "It's been fifteen minutes. Let's get in the lake."

They walked in silence through the heat. Zack kept his eyes on the ground. He wondered if Lauren had known the answer to the riddle. She must have thought him the dumbest guy alive. *Why didn't you even take a guess?* he scolded himself. And the wimpiest, too.

As they neared the lake, Zack could see the Summer Center kids climbing onto the dock. He saw Gabe's tall bunkmate applying a thick layer of sunscreen to his face, and then he spotted Gabe nearby. Gabe was smiling, his braces glinting in the sunlight, a towel draped over his shoulders.

"You guys go ahead," Zack said. "I don't feel like swimming."

"Forget those nerds," Lauren said.

"Yeah," RJ added. "Never listen to someone wearing glasses made of pencils."

Zack gave a weak laugh. "I'm okay. I'm just going to hang out here a minute. You guys should totally go swimming."

Lauren and RJ looked at each other. "Are you sure you don't want to come?" RJ asked. "It's still really hot out."

Zack looked up at their faces for the first time since the riddle. "I'm sure," he said. "Go ahead."

They hesitated, then left, and Zack sat down on a low log behind a big tree. The uneven bark dug into his legs, but it was shady, and Zack was so angry and ashamed that he wouldn't have been comfortable if he'd been sitting on a cloud. Maybe Abbot was right to complain; sharing the camp with Summer Center was totally lame. Sure, Zack sometimes wished he were smarter, that he was one of those kids who knew the answers in school without even trying, that he could keep up with Gabe. He'd gotten an 82 percent on his final exam in Social Studies, and he'd been pretty proud of himself. Gabe probably would have cried if he got an 82 percent on anything. *But Gabe's totally clueless about normal things,* Zack told himself, *like baseball cards and sports and bands.* At least, he'd thought those were normal things, until he got here. Who determined what was normal, anyway?

It was now five o'clock, and the woods became louder with footsteps and voices. Zack scooted back on his log and leaned against the tree, not wanting to talk to anyone. He closed his eyes and listened only to birds until he heard a name he couldn't ignore.

"Gabe!"

Zack sat up straight.

"Hello," he heard Gabe say.

"Get this," the first voice said. It sounded familiar, but Zack couldn't quite place it. "We were at the library, and some Senecas came by wanting to come in."

Zack held his breath. Now he recognized the voice.

"We said they could enter if they answered the riddle of the Sphinx!"

Zack heard someone snort.

"Good one!" a boy said. "That's genius."

"Did they answer it?" someone else asked.

"Are you kidding? This guy didn't even take a guess."

"It was totally over his head," one of the guards added. "Typical Seneca."

"Yeah," Gabe said. "My stepbrother goes to Camp Seneca. I bet the only riddle he knows is 'Why did the chicken cross the road?'"

Everybody laughed. Everybody except Zack.

Chapter 32

GABE

"Which is nerdier?" Wesley asked. "My You-Should-be-Studying hat, or a big glob of sunscreen on my nose?"

"The sunscreen," said Gabe.

"The hat," said Three O'Clock.

"Why not wear both," Nikhil suggested, "just to be safe?"

"Yes," Wesley agreed. "Best to be safe." He squeezed a line of sunscreen onto his nose and smeared it down the sides without rubbing it in. Then he put on a denim bucket hat that had a picture of a pointing finger and the words YOU SHOULD BE STUDYING! Finally, he hooked a new set of rubber bands into his braces.

Gabe gave him a thumbs-up. "Let's go to breakfast."

A thunderstorm had struck late the night before, so the ground outside the cabin was still damp. The air, however, was surprisingly cool and dry.

"Thank heavens!" Wesley cried. "Better weather! My glasses aren't even fogging up, it's so cool out." He splattered mud as he stepped into a wet patch of grass.

Gabe wiped the mud from his leg as he walked. "Dinner was fun last night, though," he said. The air conditioning had broken in the cafeteria, and it was too hot for the staff to cook, so a van had pulled up with boxes upon boxes of pizza. "I wonder if it's fixed, or if breakfast had to be ordered in too."

Talking about ordering breakfast in made him think of weekends at his dad's apartment. Carla often called the diner down the street and ordered breakfast on Saturday or Sunday mornings, something Gabe's own mom would never do, if there even was a way to do that on Long Island. The first time Carla said she was going to order breakfast in, Gabe thought she was joking and requested two servings of chocolate-chip pancakes. He was flabbergasted when, twenty minutes later, a delivery person buzzed the apartment and arrived with his chocolate-chip pancakes in two styrofoam containers. (Carla had laughed and given his forehead a big kiss.) One weekend, the boys woke up before their parents, so Zack found the menu in the drawer and called the diner himself to order breakfast. Gabe just stood there, staring with admiration, as Zack spoke easily into the phone, requesting scrambled eggs and toast. "Put it on our tab," he'd said. When the delivery person arrived, Zack was ready with a five-dollar tip.

Feeling a pang of homesickness, Gabe glanced to his left, hoping to catch a glimpse of Zack. The Seneca campers were circled around the flagpole as they were every morning before breakfast. Their director was standing in the center, and two small groups of kids—one of boys and one of girls— were walking toward him, preparing to raise the flag. Gabe thought he saw Zack's dark hair among the boys going to the flag, but he wasn't sure.

"Gabe?" said Three O'Clock.

Gabe saw that his bunkmates were a few steps ahead of him. He stopped looking for Zack and jogged to catch up.

"There must have been a cold front behind the storm," Nikhil said. He stopped walking, licked his finger, and held it up to feel the direction of the wind. "Yep," he said. "Coming from the northeast."

Wesley opened his arms and looked at the sky. "Thank you, weather patterns!" he sang. "Thank you, Mother Na—" His voice cracked and his praise stopped suddenly.

"What?" Nikhil asked. He looked up in the direction of Wesley's gaze and gasped.

The sound from the Senecas was getting louder. They were reciting the pledge of allegiance.

Gabe looked. Something was rising up the flagpole, only it wasn't flags. It was . . .

"Underpants!" Three O'Clock said.

Not just any underpants, Gabe realized. They were *his* underpants, the ones he'd lent Zack the first day of camp. The dinosaur briefs—with his name sewn into them.

The Senecas were so loud now that all the Summer Center campers had stopped to see what was happening. Gabe squeezed his eyes shut as tight as they would go, but that only made him hear the Seneca chant even clearer. "One NERDshion!" the Senecas shouted. "Under GEEKS! With DINOSAUR PANTIES for all!"

The whole campground seemed to erupt with laughter, and Gabe took off his glasses. He didn't want to see his own underwear flapping in the breeze. He couldn't even protest that they weren't *panties*; that would mean advertising that they belonged to him. How did the Senecas get them, anyway? How could Zack let them do this?

Wesley poked him in the shoulder. "They're pulling them down," he said.

Gabe put his glasses back on and watched as the Camp Seneca director lowered the ropes and removed the underwear. His face was red with fury and his mouth was moving, but Gabe couldn't hear what he was saying over the roar of the laughter. Some girls shrieked, and Gabe saw the formation of Senecas split like a zipper coming undone. A pair of underwear was being tossed from person to screeching person like a game of hot potato. The counselors tried to catch it, but while they focused on that, the blond boy from Zack's bunk—Abbot, Gabe remembered—sprinted away from the flagpole and tossed a couple of pairs of underwear to the girls in Amanda's bunk, who were standing near the cafeteria entrance.

"Gabe!" Jenny Chin shouted.

Gabe turned, but Jenny wasn't calling him, she was just reading the name on the label sewn into the underwear, announcing to the world whose they were.

"They're Gabe's!" another girl said, giggling.

"Yeah, they're Gabe's," Wesley shouted. "Give them back!" He ran to collect them but instead got caught up in an argument with someone from his paleontology class about whether the dinosaur on the crotch was an herbivore or carnivore.

Gabe watched Abbot run back to the Senecas and right to Zack, who he gave a high five. For a moment Gabe's eyes met Zack's. Gabe stared at him, willing his eyes to say *I trusted you* instead of spilling tears. Zack stared back, not laughing but not sympathetic either. If Gabe's telepathic powers were to be trusted, Zack's message was clear: *You deserved this.*

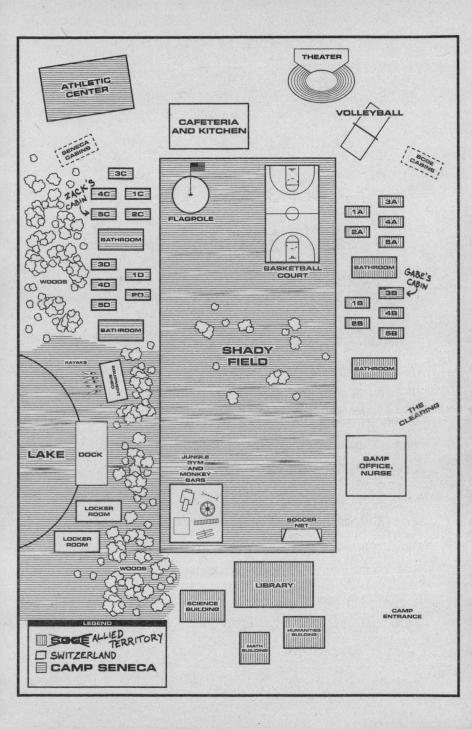

Chapter 33

ZACK

The cafeteria was buzzing during the Senecas' breakfast, even after the director announced that they'd be spending the day cleaning the campground again. It was hard to ruin a day that started with underwear going up a flagpole—as long as it was someone else's underwear.

Zack's tray was loaded with two bowls of cereal, a pile of scrambled eggs, and three pieces of toast. He thought about going to get a second tray; there was room because Abbot wasn't at the table. He was sitting with the camp director, part of an extra punishment for being the brains behind the prank. Zack had helped plan it too, and of course he'd supplied the underwear, but Abbot had taken full responsibility. "I owe you for helping me return those science cards," he told Zack. Zack found that admirable and thought maybe Abbot wasn't so bad after all, though Abbot's smirk suggested he was enjoying the notoriety.

"That underwear really caught the wind," RJ said. "It was funnier than I thought it'd be."

Zack nodded even though he was thinking the opposite—it wasn't nearly as funny as he'd anticipated. Maybe it was because Abbot had thrown the briefs to the Summer Center girls so they could read the label. That hadn't been part of the plan. Typical Abbot, always taking things a step too far. Zack had been excited to fight the nerds, assert Camp Seneca's superiority. But it was one thing to fly some nerdy underwear twenty feet in the air and another to expose whose it was.

Gabe didn't care about embarrassing me when he cracked that joke about the riddle of the Sphinx, Zack reminded himself. *Or when he floated by on a giant brain. Why should I care about embarrassing him back?*

An older kid slid into the seat normally occupied by Abbot. Zack knew he went by Franklin, though he wasn't sure if that was his first or last name. "Hey," Franklin said. "You're Zack, right?"

Zack swallowed his bite of toast and nodded.

He lowered his voice. "You supplied the underwear, right?"

Zack hesitated then nodded again.

Franklin broke into a big grin and held out his hand. "Dude, that was freaking *brilliant*!"

Zack let out his breath and shook Franklin's hand. "It wasn't totally my idea." He motioned with his chin in Abbot's direction. "My bunkmate was the one who said we should put it up the flagpole."

Franklin didn't bother looking at Abbot; he was too busy waving over some of his own friends. "Guys, this is Zack. He's the one who brought that underwear today."

All the guys nodded approvingly, and a few patted Zack on the back.

"Where'd you get that, anyway?" one of them asked. "Do you know Gavin?"

"Gabe," Zack corrected. "He's my stepbrother."

"No way!" said Franklin. "You've got, like, insider nerd information. We'll have to remember that."

"Oh wait," said one of the guys. "You're the one who dug

up the science cards. My cousin Maddie says you're cool."

They all looked at Maddie's table. She had her big sunglasses on her head and a halo of girls around her. One of them saw the boys looking, and they all began talking and looking over stealthily. Only Maddie looked directly at the boys, and she waved.

"It wasn't a big deal," Zack said, hoping his cheeks weren't red.

"You're a good guy," Franklin said. "If this nerd war gets intense, I'm glad we have you on our team." He held his fist out for a bump, then walked back to his own table, all the guys following behind him.

Zack watched them go, wondering if he shouldn't have said where he got the underwear and how much more intense the nerd war could get. He thought it'd be satisfying to embarrass Gabe after the riddle of the Sphinx. But it was kind of like that time the Space Mountain operator let him ride three times in row: As fun as it sounded, it only gave him a stomachache.

Chapter 34

GABE

Gabe might have been able to handle being the laughing stock of Camp Seneca, but it was hard to deal with being the laughing stock of Summer Center, too. Everyone looked at him with X-ray vision, knowing what was under his shorts. C^2 told him to own it, flaunt his Jurassic undies for the cause, but Gabe couldn't muster the pride. He could barely keep his arms at his sides instead of crossed in front of his pants.

His bunkmates avoided bringing it up all through breakfast, so the incident hovered like an invisible fog above the table, making everyone uncomfortable. *It'd be better if we just talked about it,* Gabe thought. Until he got to Research Methods and Amanda made an announcement. "Nobody make fun of

Gabe!" she instructed the class. "I think his underpants were cute. And very educational."

Gabe searched the floor for a trapdoor, and, not finding one, went back to wishing everyone would just pretend it never happened.

"I'm the butt of every joke," he moaned at lunch.

"You're right about *butt*," Wesley said with a giggle, then quickly covered his mouth. "Sorry."

The SCGE director stopped by the table and asked how Gabe was doing. "I've been briefed on what happened," she said. Then she paused and tried not to laugh. "Sorry."

SCGE Color War broke the morning after the flagpole incident. Gabe was picking at his cereal when smoke began to stream out of the breakfast food trays. The cafeteria workers fanned it with their aprons, which sent it whirling higher, where it bounced around the blades of the spinning ceiling fans.

At Gabe's table, Wesley was the first to notice the smoke. "What the . . ." he muttered.

Gabe looked up from his bowl, ready for the worst. Nikhil inhaled sharply, then, holding his breath, pulled his face mask out of his pocket and put it on. But before any of them could stop, drop , or roll, the smoke began changing color. At the start of the food line, above the eggs and sausages, it turned a deep shade of red. Next, by the oatmeal and hash browns, the smoke became blue. The pancakes and toast emitted green, and the cereal and milk cartons became encased in yellow.

Color War would provide a great distraction from Gabe's misery. His fingers began to tingle, but he was too nervous to let himself hope. What if this was just another Camp Seneca stunt, and the tinted smoke wasn't announcing Color War but instead poisoning his breakfast?

The loudspeakers in the cafeteria began playing a dramatic score, quietly at first, but escalating in volume. The kitchen doors opened, and four people dressed as trolls rolled in a large cauldron steaming with all four colors. They stopped in the center of the cafeteria, and every body shifted to watch. Just as the music hit a crescendo, a wizard rose from the cauldron, his arms up and outstretched with a long scepter in one and a large book in the other. He had half-round spectacles, a white beard that fell to his chest, and a robe with all four colors shimmering through the smoke.

"That's Gandalf!" Wesley said. "That's the real Gandalf from the Lord of the Rings movies!"

"Are you sure?" Nikhil asked, squinting into the smoke.

"Positive!" Wesley said. "That's him."

The music stopped abruptly, and the wizard spoke in a booming voice. "Greetings, noble citizens of Summer Center."

Now Gabe was sure Wesley was right. He was also 99 percent sure Color War was breaking, but the last 1 percent of doubt held him back from cheering along with most of the others.

"I have cast a spell on this campground," the wizard continued, "and divided you into four clans, each represented by a royal color. You will face a variety of challenges over the course of the next three days, and the clan that wins the most points will inherit the kingdom and all its powers."

The counselors filed in now—Gabe hadn't even realized they'd left—dressed like kings and queens. His own counselor, decked out in a tunic and bright yellow robe, began distributing yellow T-shirts and foam crowns. Amanda's, he saw, had her long hair in a fancy braid and was wearing a flowing red gown. She began to hand red shirts and crowns to her campers, bowing before each girl.

Gabe wanted to be excited when he put on his yellow garb. After all, Color War had been the highlight of last summer. But something just wasn't the same. Maybe it was because it was

219

an ordinary time of day (last year it had broken in the middle of the night), or maybe it was because he was on the yellow team (last year he'd been on green). Or maybe it was because he was still smarting from the humiliation of his own stepbrother running his underwear up a flagpole, and wearing a yellow crown around a campground filled with smug, nerd-hating Senecas would only make everything worse.

It was probably a combination of all those things, and Gabe wasn't the only one feeling it. The campers were cheering and clapping, but they were doing so halfheartedly, as if the very thought of Color War was exhausting. Not one team started chanting its color, and some kids didn't even bother putting on their crowns. Color War was supposed to be about team spirit, but the spirit seemed to have evaporated with the colored smoke.

So it went for the whole three days of Color War. The teams competed in water sports, *Jeopardy!*, field day, a scavenger hunt, and a sing-off. The cafeteria food was divided by color. The obstacle course featured a giant inflatable slide with various numbers printed on the sides that the campers had to multiply as they slid past, but even that wasn't as fun as it should have been. With Color War competitions in place of

SCGE's usual class schedule, the campers crossed paths with the Senecas constantly throughout the day. The people who believed they should still be flaunting their nerd pride complained that Color War wasn't academic enough. Those who didn't want to provoke the Senecas any further worried that Color War was nerdy to the nth degree. No one even seemed to be keeping track of the points, let alone determined to win.

On their walk back to their bunks after the announcement of the winners (Blue), Gabe passed Zack, and Zack called out his name. Feeling tears forming, Gabe just kept walking.

Lying in his bed later, he felt more cowardly than ever. Classes would start up again in the morning, which meant he had less than two weeks to do something heroic, and to complete a working experiment for his research question, which was how to make Summer Center fun again. So far everything he'd tried had failed on both counts. Now his Color War team had come in last place, and Summer Center had lost all the ground they'd gained against Camp Seneca. He wasn't even brave enough to face his own stepbrother without crying. If something as big and significant as Color War couldn't improve conditions at camp, what could he, one weak person, do?

Chapter 35

ZACK

"Listen up!" the camp director shouted at the end of dinner. "I have an important announcement."

Zack, who was deciding between a brownie and a blondie for dessert, put one of each on his tray and stood by the dessert bar waiting for the announcement.

"I know that relations between Camp Seneca and Summer Center have been strained," the director said.

That's one way to put it, Zack thought. The past few days, Summer Center kids had been walking around in foam crowns and wizard robes. It was like they weren't sharing the grounds with a separate camp, but rather a separate species. Yesterday morning, one of those crowns had fallen as the two camps passed each other outside the cafeteria. A Seneca girl had picked it up and returned it, and Zack heard the girls around her call her a "nerdlover." He saw that she was eating alone again tonight.

"The summer is almost over, and we don't want to go out on a bad note with our hosts," the director continued. "What better way to extend the peace pipe than by having a pow-wow?"

A powwow? Zack thought, raising his eyebrows. He thought he could hear Abbot snort from all the way across the room.

"On Saturday night, we're going to have a big campfire—with Summer Center. Everyone together!" The cafeteria grew noisy with groans and protests, but the director continued on. "We'll all gather in the woods for a fun night with music and marshmallows and, most importantly, friendship. Or at least civility. Since Summer Center has been nice enough to host us this summer, we are going to be their hosts for the camp-fire. We'll spend the week preparing, so choose your activities with that in mind. Arts and crafts will make decorations and invitations, drama and music will prepare some entertain-ment, and cooking will provide some of the food."

What? Zack thought. This was the second-to-last week of cooking, and Zig had said it'd be protein week: chicken, fish, and beef. Even with his limited menu-planning experience, Zack knew they wouldn't be serving proteins at a campfire for hundreds of kids. That meant they'd probably have to spend the week making something stupid and easy, like—he looked down at his plate—brownies or blondies. Lame.

"What a waste of our last Saturday night," Abbot said when Zack returned to the table. "We have hardly any camp left, and we have to spend half of it preparing to hang out with *them*."

Ignoring Abbot, RJ asked if Zack was going to eat both of his desserts. Zack shrugged and told RJ to pick one. After selecting the blondie and swallowing a big bite of it, RJ said, "It's cool you get to cook for everyone."

"Kind of," Zack said. Abbot usually made some crack about Betty Crocker when Zack talked about cooking, so he didn't bring up his disappointment about the displacement of protein week.

Franklin came over to Zack's table and nodded hello. "What's up, Zack?" he said.

Zack sat up a little straighter. "Hey," he said.

"What a waste of our last Saturday night, huh?" Abbot repeated for Franklin.

"Maybe not," Franklin said. "The guys and I were just saying, we think it's more like an opportunity."

"What do you mean?" Zack asked.

"We have to share our campfire with the nerds," Franklin explained, "but since we'll all be in the same place, this is our chance to really get them one last time. Here's our chance to go out with a bang."

"Oh yeah!" Abbot said. "We can really get them."

"Yeah, man," Franklin said with a chuckle at Abbot. Then he turned back to Zack. "Since your brother goes to SCGE, we thought you might have some stuff we can use, like that underwear."

"I don't know," Zack admitted. "I haven't talked to Gabe all summer." *And he wouldn't even look at me when I tried to apologize,* he added to himself.

"That's all right," Franklin said. "You don't have to come up with anything on the spot. But you should help us plan, at least. Since you've got insight into the nerd brain."

"Yeah," Abbot said. "We'll come up with something good, like when me and Maddie and Leo stole those science cards."

Franklin looked at Abbot for a long moment, as though

sizing him up. Apparently finding him all right, he said, "Okay, dude." Then he punched Zack lightly in the arm. "See you later, Zack. Let me know if you think of anything."

"Later," Zack said.

Franklin walked away, stopping to cough "nerdlover" by the girl who'd returned the crown yesterday, then going to his own table. Zack wasn't the only one watching Franklin—so was every girl in Lauren and Maddie's bunk. Then their faces went back, stopping to look, impressed, at Zack and his bunkmates. Lauren caught Zack's eye, then raised one eyebrow and gave a half smile, her dimple visible even from so far away.

Zack waved to her and turned back to his brownie, thinking about what he might cook up for the campfire, both for Zig and for Franklin.

"What's a staple campfire food?" Zig asked his cooking protégées the next day.

"S'mores?" Lauren guessed.

"Yes!" Zig said, extending his tattooed arm out for a fist bump. "S'mores. And what's the best part of s'mores?"

"The chocolate," Lauren said at the same time Zack said, "Melting the marshmallows."

"The way the chocolate melts because of the melted marshmallow," Lauren amended. Zack rolled his eyes at her, and she punched him in the shoulder.

Zig considered. "I'd say those are all good things. Which is why we're going to elevate that campfire classic to fine cuisine. We're going to make fondue."

A few of the chefs-in-training began to whisper excitedly, but Zack had no idea what fondue was. He hoped it tasted better than it sounded.

"'Fondue' comes from the French verb 'to melt,'" Zig explained. "Traditionally, it's a pot of melted cheese with stuff to dip into it: pieces of chicken, vegetables, bread."

Zack instantly thought of the cheese fries he always ate at Coney Island. Zig was helping him develop sophisticated tastes, but the memory of soft, greasy fries dipped in neon-orange cheese made his stomach growl. He and Gabe had shared an extra-large order a few weeks before they'd left for camp, and they'd taken turns using their last fries to swipe every ounce of cheese, until the fries were just pieces of mush in their fingers and the paper bowl was smudged spotless.

"We'll make some cheese fondue," Zig said, "but we'll also make some chocolate fondue."

"Like, melted chocolate?" Zack asked, all thoughts of cheese fries being replaced by something even more delicious.

"Exactly," Zig said. "Pots of melted chocolate that you can drizzle onto a marshmallow."

Zack tapped his fingers together. Who needed protein week? Chocolate fondue sounded downright spectacular.

When Zack related the cooking plan that night before lights-out, RJ moaned and fell back onto his mattress. "Roasted marshmallows with melted chocolate?" he repeated, incredulous. "Dude. Talk about heaven."

"I know," Zack said. "We'll have all these big pots at various stations, and they'll be kept warm with fires, and you can dip stuff into them, or drizzle it on with a spoon."

"Drizzle? How about drench?" RJ said. "Can you reserve an entire pot for just me?"

"Yeah," Zack said with a laugh. "I'll hide a pot behind a tree or something, and you'll be the only one who knows where it is."

"Big pots of melted chocolate?" Abbot asked, sliding out of his bed and looking up at Zack.

"Yeah," Zack said. "And ones with cheese."

Abbot slapped the side of bed. "Get ready to have your

mind blown," he said. "A big pot of melted chocolate is perfect for hiding stuff. You can mark certain pots for the nerds to use, and mixed in with the chocolate can be other stuff. They won't know what hit them!"

"What sort of stuff?" Zack asked, skeptical.

"Bugs, spiders . . ." Abbot looked out the window, his eyes shining with possibility. "Dirt, mud . . . urine!"

"That's disgusting," RJ said. He rolled over, away from the conversation.

"Don't turn nerdlover on us," Abbot warned.

"Dude!" said Zack. "There's no way I'm putting *urine* in my food."

"Fine," Abbot said, "but we could put other stuff. Just to gross them out. Or—wait, I've got it. How about that hot pepper you told us about, Zack? The ones that are a million times hotter than a jalapeño."

"Ghost chilies?"

"Yeah! Ghost chilies!" Abbot said. "You said there's one in the kitchen, right? You just mix some in with the chocolate. The nerds will think their brains are going to catch on fire. And we'll hide all the water!"

Zack looked across the top bunk at RJ, who rolled back

over and shook his head in disbelief. Maybe he never should have mentioned the ghost chilies to Abbot. But at least spiking the fondue with hot pepper was better than doing it with urine, which he didn't doubt for one gross second that Abbot would help him procure.

"I don't know," Zack said, remembering the burn in his mouth after biting that jalapeño and trying to mentally multiply it by hundreds. "What if Camp Seneca people eat it by mistake?"

"It's okay if nerdlovers eat it," Abbot said with a laugh. "But you'll be cooking, so you can mark the pots somehow. Between us and Maddie and Franklin, we can spread the word about which ones are for nerds only." Abbot pushed his hair from his face and smiled in admiration of himself. "I'll tell Franklin about it," he said. "His friends are going to flip out."

Franklin, Zack thought. He knew Franklin would find it pretty funny. It wouldn't be too hard to do. And it wasn't like ghost chilies were toxic, just hot. "It would be kind of funny," Zack admitted.

"It'd be freakin' hilarious," Abbot corrected. "You guys are lucky to have me here. I'm so smart, I should switch camps."

Chapter 36

GABE

"A campfire with all the Senecas?" Wesley said. "What a waste of a Saturday night."

Nikhil frowned as he looked at the invitation. The director had announced the campfire at dinner, and their counselor had given each of them an invitation when they'd returned to their bunks. "How did the director approve this? Hasn't she ever read *Romeo & Juliet*? Or watched *West Side Story*? Bad things happen when enemy groups meet on a Saturday night."

"You're right," said Wesley, suddenly nervous. "People fall in love across enemy lines."

"Right," said Nikhil. "And then they get killed."

Three O'Clock's eyes grew round.

Gabe patted Nikhil on the shoulder. "I don't think anybody's going to die."

"Even with your stepbrother doing the cooking?" Wesley said with a snort. "Just kidding."

"Believe me," Gabe said, shaking his head, "I'm just as surprised as you are." He looked again at the invitation. It said YOU'RE INVITED! at the top in cheery bubble letters, and the details were printed in a neat hand. And at the bottom, surrounded by stars and drawings of marshmallows on sticks, was a list of the *Camp Seneca chefs* who'd be making *delicious fondue!* There were eight names listed, and Zack's was one of them.

Gabe never saw Zack do anything in the kitchen besides open the fridge or pantry for a store-bought snack. He wondered if Zack had gotten in trouble for the underwear incident, and having to cook for the campfire was his punishment. The concept of Zack *choosing* to make fondue just did not compute.

"Do you think they're planning to attack us at this campfire?" Nikhil asked, looking thoughtfully at the territory map on their wall. "To officially claim the entire campus for Camp Seneca before the summer ends?"

"Yes," said Three O'Clock.

Wesley snapped his fingers. "We should get them first!"

"I don't know," Nikhil said with a sigh. "Nothing we've tried to do so far has worked. No offense, Gabe."

Gabe nodded to show there was none taken. He knew better than anyone that all his attempts had failed.

"We just haven't figured it out yet, right, Gabe?" said Wesley. "It's like you were teaching us about research methods. You rarely get the results you expect on the first try."

"That's true," Gabe granted. "You have to change your experiment, or maybe even adjust your theory, as you go."

"Yeah!" Wesley said. "So we can still win this. Right, Three O'Clock?"

Three O'Clock shrugged.

Gabe perked up. Maybe they were right, and he should follow his own advice and not let one mortifying event keep him down. There might even still be time to do something heroic. He got out his Heroes binder and flipped through his notes. He didn't have any superpowers, so none of the comic-book heroes he'd studied were any help. And he was going to a campfire, not a trial, so he couldn't be a heroic lawyer, like Atticus Finch. He looked back at real heroes from history. "Gandhi went on a hunger strike," he offered. "We could all refuse to eat their food."

"They'd probably be happy about that," Nikhil said. "More food for them."

"And fondue *is* delicious," Wesley said.

"What is fondue?" Three O'Clock asked.

Wesley looked out the window as though there were a pot of it dangling from the trees, just out of reach. "It's melty, cheesy, chocolately heaven. With sticks."

Three O'Clock wrinkled his forehead.

"Fondue," Nikhil defined. "From the French for 'to melt.' It's a pot of chocolate or cheese into which you dip food."

"How do you dip in chocolate? Or cheese?" Three O'Clock asked.

"The chocolate's melted," Gabe explained. "So it's soft. Kind of like"—he tried to think of something with a similar consistency that Three O'Clock would know—"cytoplasm."

"Yeah!" said Nikhil. "I was going to say soup, but cytoplasm is more accurate."

Three O'Clock said, "Ah!" He put up a finger, then shuffled

around under his bed until he came up with a plastic container. He pulled open the lid and took out a goopy ball of green slime. "Cytoplasm!" he announced.

"Oh my gosh," said Wesley. "That is amazing! Have you had that under your bed all summer, just waiting for the perfect moment to take it out?"

Three O'Clock nodded.

Gabe asked if he could touch some of the cytoplasm, and Three O'Clock held out the container. It was cold and kind of sticky, though it slid between his fingers with surprising momentum. He had to catch a big glop of it before it hit the floor.

Nikhil asked if he could touch some of the cytoplasm too. "We made some of this in my chemistry class last summer. It's really part of molecular biology, but my teacher thought it was fun," he said. "It's easy to make, too. And it's nontoxic, so it's perfectly safe. I made sure before handling it last year."

"Do you think there's still stuff to make it in the chemistry rooms?" Wesley asked.

"Probably," Nikhil said. "I know my same teacher is teaching it again this summer."

Wesley smiled slowly. "You guys," he said. "This is it. This is our way to get Camp Seneca at the campfire. We replace some of the fondue with cytoplasm. They'll think they're going to eat some chocolatey goodness, but instead they'll be making cytoplasm-covered marshmallows!"

"Won't they realize it before dipping?" Gabe asked. "This doesn't exactly look like chocolate. Or cheese."

"Well, yeah, because it's green. But some brown or yellow food coloring will make it look close enough that they'll dip unknowingly."

"Or," Gabe said, the gears in his head starting to turn, "we could just tint the top somehow, so when they dip something in deeper, they come up with green cytoplasm by surprise."

Even Nikhil was considering it. "It would be a victory. And if we make it the way we did in chemistry, it's not going to actually hurt anyone."

"Yes!" Wesley said. He began pacing in the space between the beds. "The details will take some figuring out. Like when we'll make it and how we'll get it into the pots."

"And how we'll make sure everyone at Summer Center knows about it so *they* don't get slimed," Nikhil pointed out.

"C^2 is going to love this! With the combined IQ of the Sssquad," Wesley said, "I'm sure we can pull it off. We'll all be heroes!"

* * *

The Sssquad immediately liked Operation: Cytoplasm, and plans began taking shape the next day at recess. "This is our last chance," C² said, putting his arms around Gabe and Wesley. "Everyone at Summer Center is counting on us. With this plan, we'll take down the Senecas once and for all."

But ever since Wesley had used the word "hero," Gabe wasn't so sure. During free time, he was supposed to go with Wesley, Nikhil, and C² to find the cytoplasm ingredients. He told them he wasn't feeling well, and that they should go without him. It wasn't a total lie; as mad as he was at Zack, his stomach turned over every time he thought about his stepbrother spending hours cooking up fondue, only to have it turned into geeky green slime.

Nikhil insisted that someone stay with Gabe, just to be safe. Since Nikhil was the one who knew how to make cytoplasm and Wesley didn't want to miss out, that someone was Three O'Clock. The two of them lay on their beds in silence for a while, but then Gabe decided he'd rather be outside. He took his binders for both Research Methods and Heroes, and Three O'Clock took his latest batch of letters from home, and they found a quiet part of the woods with no Senecas and a long log to share.

As Gabe looked over his Research Methods notes, he figured out one thing that was holding him back. All his previous experiments to make Summer Center fun had failed, and Operation: Cytoplasm was more of the same. It didn't adjust his hypothesis; it didn't even take previous results into account. It just assumed that a variation on the same experiment—battling Senecas with over-the-top nerdiness—would achieve a different outcome. When in fact, maybe Summer Center would get ahead for another brief period, but then Camp Seneca would get them back, and things would be exactly the same, if not even worse.

"What do you think of the cytoplasm plan?" Gabe asked Three O'Clock.

Three looked up from his mail. "Is kind of funny," he said.

"Yes," Gabe agreed. "But do you think it will work? Like, do you think it'll make us win against Camp Seneca?"

"Win?" Three O'Clock said. "What is there to win?"

Gabe cocked his head. That was a deep question. He thought they were trying to win the campground, to defend their right to be smart, but the battle had gone beyond that, hadn't it? Now it was personal, brother against brother, and he didn't even know what they were fighting about.

"You're right," Gabe said. "I don't think ruining the fondue is going to make the Senecas be nice to us, or make camp more fun." *And it definitely won't make things okay between me and Zack after camp ends,* he realized.

Three O'Clock shook his head. "No one will win."

Three O'Clock went back to the letter he was writing, and Gabe went back to his Research Methods binder. If attacking again wasn't the right approach, what was? With all the types of experiments he'd studied, none of them seemed appropriate.

He sighed and switched to looking at Heroes. Every single hero knew what he was fighting for. "You know what, Three?" Gabe said. "Heroes are heroes because they're fighting for something they think is so important, they're willing to risk *everything* for it. They'll do whatever it takes."

"Yes," Three O'Clock said. "They know what they want."

Gabe looked at him for a long moment. He thought about C^2, who had said all Summer Center was counting on him. Then he thought about Zack, who might be in the kitchen cooking fondue. *What do I want to fight for?* he asked himself.

Three went back to writing his letter.

"Who are you writing to?" Gabe asked.

"My twin sister," Three O'Clock said, his lips turning up involuntarily.

"I didn't know you had a twin sister," Gabe said.

"Yes. She is in Seoul."

"Do you miss her?" Gabe asked.

Three laughed. "I did not think I would," he said. "But yes."

Gabe laughed too. Maybe there was one experiment—something totally different—that was worth a try. "I think I'm going to write a letter to my stepbrother," he said.

Three O'Clock nodded. "I think that is a good idea."

Chapter 37

ZACK

The note was sticking out the top of Zack's baseball-card binder, which was in a drawer with a mass of balled-up T-shirts. Zack hadn't taken out his cards all week, and he wouldn't have even looked in there if he hadn't splattered practice fondue on his shirt and needed to change it. He had to move the binder to reach the shirt he wanted, and there was the paper poking out with his name written in handwriting that was at once shocking and familiar. Zack gasped and pulled it out quickly.

Zack,

Any chance for a truce? Meet me Thursday at 10 p.m.

in the woods by the snake spot.

-Gabe

p. s. This is for real. It's not a trick.

Zack folded the note and looked around, making sure Abbot wasn't anywhere nearby. Then he unfolded it and read it again. *A truce,* he thought. The word seemed to come from a faraway land. Between Abbot's ghost chili idea and Franklin's endorsement of it and Maddie's trying to impress Zack by putting his name (and all the chefs') on the invitations she'd helped design, the Senecas were counting on Zack more than ever. What would happen to his reputation if he met with one of the Summer Center campers and called a truce? "Nerdlover" wouldn't begin to describe it.

"What's that?"

Startled, Zack gripped the note so hard he almost crushed it. But it was just RJ. "Oh hey," he said.

RJ raised his eyebrows. "You okay?"

"Yeah," Zack said. "I was just about to change my shirt."

Still holding the note in his right hand, he pointed to the fondue stain with his left.

RJ nodded, got a candy bar out of his drawer, and sat down on the unused bottom bed to eat it. "Are you really going to do Abbot's hot-pepper idea?" he asked.

Zack paused with his head in his clean shirt. Then he pushed it through the hole. "I don't know," he said. "What do you think about the whole thing?"

RJ shrugged one shoulder and sighed. "To be honest," he said, "I'm pretty tired of Abbot and his nerd war. I don't really know what he's trying to prove."

Zack let his fist with the crushed note open slightly, and eased himself down on Abbot's bed, opposite RJ. He hadn't really thought about it as being *Abbot's* nerd war. He'd thought it was all of Camp Seneca's. "I guess we've been trying to prove that this camp is ours."

RJ shrugged again and took a big bite of his candy bar. "But it's not," he said while chewing. "I mean, for this summer, it was both of ours. But really, it's theirs."

Zack thought about last summer, when he'd come to pick up Gabe on the last day. At that point, he hadn't known that this was a camp for smart kids; all he knew was that Gabe loved it and had savored every second of his six weeks there. Zack had been so jealous, he wanted to go to a camp of his own.

"You probably know better than anyone," RJ continued. "Your stepbrother must have been pretty angry when he found out they'd have to share their camp with us."

Zack leaned back on the wall and cocked his head. *He'd* been angry when he learned he'd be sharing the campground with Gabe, but he'd never even considered what Gabe might have thought. Could it be that RJ was right, that Gabe just wanted to enjoy his nerd heaven without any intruders?

He suddenly realized that Gabe never had other friends hang out with them when Zack went to visit him, not even for his birthday. *Is Gabe embarrassed that I'm his stepbrother?* Zack wondered with a pang of hurt. *Is* that *why I haven't seen him all summer?* If so, it must have taken a lot for him to propose a truce. If Zack didn't accept it—if he went along with Abbot's plan—it was only going to make things worse. Here and at home.

Zack sat up, opened his hand, and held the note out to RJ. "I found this in my drawer. It's from my stepbrother."

RJ read it over and looked up with his mouth slightly open. He glanced automatically at the bunk entrance to make sure Abbot wasn't coming. "You think it's for real?" he whispered.

Zack nodded. "I trust him."

"Are you going to go? I think you should go."

Zack realized he'd already known the answer, but RJ's opinion confirmed it. "Yes."

Chapter 38

GABE

Gabe lay awake in his bed, glasses on, staring at the ceiling and trying to analyze the breathing rates of his bunkmates to see if they were up. Wesley was notorious for conking out quickly and sleeping heavily—so heavily, he didn't wake himself despite all his sleeptalking and rolling around—and his slow, even breaths suggested that tonight was no different. Nikhil, on the other hand, drifted off more slowly and, Gabe assumed, carefully. His breaths were harder to hear, since Gabe was right above him, but the fact that Gabe hadn't felt him shift at all in at least ten minutes made him think that Nikhil was asleep. Three O'Clock snored a little, and he wasn't snoring now, but he knew about Gabe's meeting, so it didn't matter if he was up. In fact, Gabe hoped he was up. He could use some reassurance before sneaking out to the woods at ten p.m. What if Zack didn't show up? What if Zack *did* show up and accept the truce? How would the Sssquad react when they found out he'd canceled their opportunity to take down the Senecas?

When the light on his watch showed that it was 9:52, Gabe lifted the side of his sleeping bag (he hadn't zipped it, so that he wouldn't have to make noise unzipping it) and rotated his legs over the edge of his bed. He grasped the flashlight he'd put in his sleeping bag, and slowly, methodically climbed down the ladder until his bare feet touched the cold floor. Wesley mumbled something unintelligible and rolled over. Nikhil stayed still and silent. Gabe held his breath, took his sweatshirt from where it hung on the bedpost, and unhooked his night brace and hung it there instead. Then he picked up his flip-flops from the top of his dresser. He'd put them on when he got outside.

As he tiptoed out of the room, Three O'Clock whispered, "Good luck. If anyone asks, I will say you needed to use the toilet."

"Thanks," Gabe whispered back.

"I hope he comes."

"Me too."

Flip-flops, flashlight, and sweatshirt in hand, Gabe tiptoed the length of the cabin. He had chosen ten p.m. because he figured the counselors would still be hanging out at that time, but he allowed himself to exhale in relief when he saw that he had been right—his counselor wasn't in his room.

Outside, Gabe slid his feet into his sandals and put on his sweatshirt, but he didn't dare turn on his flashlight until he was farther from the cabins. The last, and only, time he'd snuck out after lights-out, it was a year ago, and he'd been about to kayak to Dead Man's Island. Even though this time he was only meeting his stepbrother in the woods, he wasn't any less nervous. What if his counselor saw him? What if there were strange nocturnal creatures in the woods? What if it was all for nothing because Zack wasn't going to show up?

When he was about halfway across the field, Gabe heard the squeak of a cabin door. Unsure whether to freeze or sprint the rest of the way into the woods, Gabe did neither—he turned around. A silhouette appeared in the light outside the door of the cabin next to his. Even in the darkness and at this distance, Gabe recognized its halo of hair. He shook his head. *It figures,* he thought.

Amanda jogged across the woods until she met Gabe. His eyes adjusting to the dark, Gabe thought he saw her smile. "Where are you going?" Amanda asked loudly.

"Shh!" Gabe hissed. He walked the rest of the field briskly with Amanda at his side. Even though he only stared straight ahead and tried to convey his annoyance, he could sense her excitement at the adventure.

Only when they reached the woods and were safely hidden from the cabins by a few rows of trees did Gabe stop and face her. "What are you doing?"

"What are *you* doing?"

"I asked you first," Gabe said.

"I asked *you* first. On the field."

Gabe crossed his arms. There was no winning with her.

"Are you trying to do something heroic?" Amanda asked.

"Maybe," Gabe said. "I'm going to meet my stepbrother."

Amanda smiled. "I thought so. It has to do with Operation: Cytoplasm, right?"

"How did you know?" Gabe said, and he could see Amanda's smile getting bigger. "What are *you* doing?" he demanded.

249

"I need to do something heroic too, you know," Amanda said. "My heroic act is making sure you're not doing something stupid, and stopping you if you are."

Gabe blinked into the shadows. Amanda always had a cockeyed way of looking at things, but her act of heroism was somehow flattering. He knew he was blushing, and he hoped her eyes hadn't adjusted to the dark enough to tell. "Thanks," he said sincerely. "But I don't think what I'm doing is stupid. I'm trying to broker a truce."

"I agree it's not stupid," Amanda said after a moment. "I've changed my heroic act to be helping you broker a truce."

She took a step deeper into the woods, but Gabe touched her arm. "Thanks," he said again, "but I'm meeting my step-brother, and I haven't spoken to him all summer. I kind of want to do it alone."

"Do you want me to stay back here in case you need me? You can shine your flashlight three times as a distress signal."

Gabe considered. It was tempting to have some backup in case Zack was going to ambush him with other Senecas, or to have a partner to sneak back with if Zack didn't show up. But something told him neither of those things would happen, and Zack would be there, on his own, ready to talk.

Gabe lit up the time on his watch: 10:01. "That's okay," he said. "I'll be all right. But if we make a plan that requires extra people, I'll let you know."

"All right," Amanda said. She placed one hand on Gabe's shoulder, leaned in, and gave him a kiss on the cheek. "Good luck."

Gabe's eyes sprung open and his feet bore into the ground. He stayed stationary like that, listening to the leaves crinkle as Amanda ran back toward the field. The sound stopped suddenly, and Amanda called, "Hey, Gabe. Will you vouch for me that I did something heroic?"

Gabe shook himself and wiggled his tingling fingers. "Yes," he said into the distance, his voice squeaking just a little. "I will."

Chapter 39

ZACK

The place in the woods Gabe meant wasn't marked in any way, but Zack knew exactly where it was. Every time he'd passed it all summer, he could picture the snake they'd encountered on the log, slithering up and darting its thin tongue in and out. Sneaking out of the cabin had been easy, but he was nervous waiting here now, too nervous to sit on a log or lean against a tree. So he just stood, awkwardly, waiting.

He turned in the direction of the approaching footsteps, praying they were Gabe's. A flashlight beam traveled along the ground, nearing Zack and finally illuminating his sandals, then his legs in his pajama pants. The light traveled up until it hit his face. He lifted his hand and said, "Whoa, hey."

Gabe turned the light on himself, shining it up under his chin like he was about to tell a spooky story. "Hey!"

Zack grinned, a rush of warmth surging from his head down. He hadn't realized how much he'd wanted to see Gabe until he actually saw him.

It was awkward for a minute—Zack didn't know if they were supposed to hug or shake hands or something—and they both just stood there smiling at each other like goofs. Gabe's face was flushed and he looked kind of shell-shocked, which Zack figured was from him running there. Or maybe he was nervous because he was still angry about the underwear. It was probably best for Zack to clear the air, but what should he say?

Gabe spoke before Zack could decide. "Are you cooking fondue?"

"Yeah!" he replied. "I've kind of gotten really into cooking. It's really fun, and the cooking instructor is this guy named Zig, who's really awesome." Zack stopped himself from rambling and saying "really" again. "Yes. I'm one of the people making fondue for the campfire."

Gabe used his flashlight to find his way onto a log. He shined it on Zack, then on the log, then back on his own face, which seemed to be asking if Zack wanted to sit. Not wanting to appear a wimp, Zack made his way to the log and sat down too. What were the chances, really, that they'd be joined by a snake?

Gabe flicked off the flashlight. "The Sssquad has this plan," he said, "to sabotage your fondue."

"The squad?"

"The Save Summer Center Squad," Gabe explained. "We organized the parade."

Zack didn't comment on the parade or the Save Summer Center Squad. It was probably best to keep things about the future. "Some Seneca people have a plan too. They want me to put this really hot chili in the fondue."

Gabe's mouth opened in a half smile. "Our plan is to replace the fondue with cytoplasm."

Zack had no idea what cytoplasm was, but it didn't sound good. "Dude," he said. "Why does everyone want to mess with my fondue?"

Gabe looked at him and laughed.

Zack looked at Gabe and laughed.

Gabe laughed harder, which made Zack laugh harder. Soon, they were both laughing so hard that they were doubled over on the log.

"Shh," Gabe said, his shoulders still shaking.

But neither could get it together. And right then, laughing with his stepbrother on a log in the woods in the middle of the night, Zack didn't care if the camp director found them.

"All right," Gabe whispered, catching his breath. "So, I don't really want to make you guys eat cytoplasm."

"And I don't really want to make you guys eat ghost chili peppers."

"Ghost chili peppers? That sounds scary."

"Psycho plasma sounds scary too."

"Cytoplasm," Gabe corrected. "It's the gel-like stuff that fills a cell. But we're not making real cytoplasm. We're making a green slime that kind of resembles it."

Green slime? Zack was insulted. He was making fondue, not slime. "You can eat green slime?"

"It's not toxic," Gabe said, "but it probably doesn't taste very good. The recipe is from molecular biology."

Zack sprung up from the log. "Molecular gastronomy!" he said a little too loudly.

Gabe stood up too and put a finger to his lips. "Molecular *biology*," he whispered.

"No, I'm talking about molecular *gastronomy*. It's this cool way of cooking where you make stuff that tastes good but has all sorts of weird textures, like spheres or gels." He jumped over the log and back. This was going to be perfect. "Can you get the psycho plasma recipe from your friends? Zig can help us make it really gel-like but taste awesome, and we can serve it at the campfire. It'll be, like, a peace offering to the nerds—I mean, a peace offering for Summer Center." *And from me to you*, Zack thought, but he didn't say it for risk of sounding cheesy.

"A peace offering?" Gabe asked, adjusting his glasses.

"Yeah," Zack said. He cleared his throat and declared officially: "As Camp Seneca's gift to Summer Center, we chefs will prepare a delicious, psycho plasma–like gel."

"Cytoplasm."

"Cytoplasm. But in return, you guys have got to cool it on the Nerd Pride stuff and let us enjoy our last week at camp."

Gabe closed his eyes and thought about it. "Okay," he said with a nod. "I will present it to the Sssquad. We'll back off, as long as this really will be peace, and you'll respect our kind of fun too."

"Gabe," Zack said, "we're making you gel-like stuff from *cells*." He held out his hand, but Gabe held his back.

"What are you going to do about the ghost chilies?" Gabe asked.

Zack sat back down. *Franklin and them are looking forward to someone eating one of the world's hottest peppers. . . .* He felt another brilliant idea taking shape; being around Gabe was like fuel for his brain. He gave a mischievous smile. "I think I know what to do with that, too."

Chapter 40

GABE

Gabe was nervous about presenting the peace offering to the Sssquad, but it helped that he went into the meeting with Three O'Clock and Amanda already on his side.

"I know that Operation: Cytoplasm would have been successful in the short term," he said, standing at the head of the picnic table at which the Sssquad was convened on Thursday during recess. "But it would have been just another battle in an ongoing war. They were planning to get us again at the campfire too. This way, we strike a peace agreement that allows us to retain our territory *and* eat cytoplasm—only it should actually taste good."

Amanda stood up from her place at the end of the table. "Gabe was very brave to broker this deal. We learned in Heroes that sometimes the most heroic thing you can do is choose not to fight." She sat back down.

Gabe flushed and looked up at the trees. He could still feel the spot on his cheek where Amanda's lips had been just fourteen hours ago.

Nikhil scratched his head through his tall hair. "You snuck out last night and made this peace treaty, all by yourself?"

"He did," Wesley answered, crossing his arms. "I can't believe you didn't tell us."

"I'm sorry," Gabe said. He knew that Nikhil was thinking of his safety and Wesley was annoyed at not being invited along, and he truly was sorry for both reasons. "I was meeting with my stepbrother, and I didn't even know if he'd show up, let alone accept a truce. I thought it'd be best to keep it a secret until it was done." He glanced at Three O'Clock, hoping he wouldn't give away that he had known ahead of time. But Three had the best poker face Gabe had ever seen. Among other things, Gabe was realizing, Three O'Clock was great at keeping secrets. He wondered what else was locked in Three's vault. "I didn't officially accept the offering," Gabe added. "I just told Zack that I'd present it to the Sssquad."

"I think we should accept it," Jenny Chin said, hitting the table with both hands. "It'll be more fun to eat the cytoplasm than to make the Senecas eat it."

"I concur," Amanda said.

"I concur squared," Nikhil said. "But I propose we get the treaty in writing, just to be safe."

Wesley sighed and slumped on his bench. "I concur cubed, I guess. But only because I care about the greater good of all of Summer Center."

Serafina voted that they still sabotage the campfire. "Now they *really* won't be expecting it," she explained. "In the words of our anthem, 'We nerds will rule the world.'"

Three O'Clock shook his head and sided with Gabe.

C^2's friend said that Serafina was right.

Everyone looked at C^2, who'd been silently taking in the whole meeting. Gabe gulped, praying he would vote for the truce, even if he considered Gabe a traitor to Nerd Pride. If C^2 wanted to go ahead with the sabotage, Gabe would have to find the strength to refuse. It'd be hard to go against the Sssquad, but he couldn't betray his brother.

C^2 was silent. He sat watching a squirrel climb a tree and disappear.

Jenny rolled her eyes. "He does this sometimes," she said. "My mom says he's lost in thought, but I think he's just being weird."

"C^2?" Gabe asked nervously. "Are the terms of the peace agreeable to you?"

"Yes," C^2 said, turning to Gabe suddenly and looking him right in the eye. "Well done."

Chapter 41

ZACK

"Chocolate fondue team!" Zig called. "You guys coming along?"

"Yes, chef."

"Cheese fondue," Zig said. "Status?"

"Almost ready, chef."

"Sour-apple cytoplasm team?"

"Taking it out of the fridge now," Lauren answered.

Zig waited at the counter while Lauren and Zack got one tray of gelifying cytoplasm out of the refrigerator. Zack knew he was as curious to see how it was turning out as they were. When Zack had presented Zig with the idea and the images of cells that Gabe had given him for inspiration, Zig had thought it was a brilliant foray into molecular gastronomy. "You're really thinking like a chef," Zig had said, and Zack hadn't been able to shake a silly smile the whole rest of the day.

Now it was Saturday, a few hours before the campfire, and the cooking crew was working extra hard to finish their preparations in time. They'd been making trial fondues all week, but it had taken a couple of days for Zig to come up with a cytoplasm recipe and procure the ingredients, so there'd been no time for a practice run.

"It's green," Zack said. And it was. They'd used apples, kiwis, and lime juice to make the cytoplasm, and the result was a bright green gel that jiggled as Lauren carried it over. She set it down on the counter, and Zig handed Zack a spoon.

"The brains behind the concept gets the first taste," he said.

Zack took the spoon proudly. Who would have thought he'd be "the brains" behind anything, especially when Gabe was around? He dipped the spoon into the tray and paused with the bite outside his mouth.

"Try it!" Lauren said, poking him with her finger.

Zack put the spoon in his mouth. And there it was, the reason he loved cooking. "It's really good!" he announced. He put his spoon back in the gel and took another bite. It was cold and zesty and just the right degree of sour, and the consistency was surprising to his tongue, but in a good way. And *he'd* made it!

Zig handed Lauren a spoon and kept one for himself. Lauren's face lit up as she ate her spoonful. When she finished it, she threw her arms around Zack.

Zig nodded as he swallowed, then held out his hand for high fives. "Cooking requires a lot of technique," he said, "but when it comes down to it, it's all about heart. The Summer Center kids are going to freakin' love this. You should be really proud of yourselves."

Zack stood there beaming, and he let his arm stay around Lauren's back even though they were done hugging.

"But you've got a lot of work to do still," Zig said, clapping his hands once. "We've got to make these look like cells, right? The cookie cutters are over there. Cut out a circle and place it on one of these plates. Then add the slice of kiwi for the"—he pulled a printed-out picture of a cell from his back pocket and unfolded it—"nucleus, and the dots of whipped cream for the . . . mito . . . mitock . . . whatever these blobs are called."

"Mitochondria," Lauren said. "They produce energy for the cell."

Zack looked at her with his eyebrows raised.

"What?" she said with a coy smile. "There are smart people who don't go to Summer Center."

Zig gave her another high five before leaving to check on the other dishes.

Zack and Lauren set to work cutting the cytoplasm into circles and making individual cells on plates. Zack couldn't wait to see Gabe's reaction. He'd realized, lying in his bed after their meeting the other night, that he hadn't actually apologized for the underwear stuff. He was going to say something when Gabe met him to tell him the truce was a deal, and to give him the pictures of cytoplasm, but he'd chickened out. He hoped that these molecular-gastronomical cells would make up for anything Gabe might still be holding against him.

"These look perfect," Lauren said as they finished preparing the last of the cells.

"They really do," Zack agreed. "I can put them all in the fridge. Why don't you go chill out before dinner?"

"Are you sure? I can help put them away."

"Nah, I got it. I'll see you at the campfire."

Lauren gave him a suspicious look. "You're not planning

something mean, are you? Something else you'll have to apologize for with molecular gastronomy?"

That stung, but Zack kept his gaze innocent. After a few seconds, Lauren shrugged and took off her apron. "See you tonight," she said before heading out.

"Later." Zack started to move plates with cells into the refrigerator, keeping one eye on the door. Once he was sure Lauren was gone and wasn't coming back, he stopped and looked up at the plastic bag marked *DANGER: DO NOT HANDLE*. He checked out the kitchen again. One of the girls who'd made the chocolate fondue was scraping it into containers, and Zig was busy helping put final touches on the cheese fondue.

Now's your chance, Zack thought, imagining Abbot. He casually slipped on a pair of dishwashing gloves and reached for the bag with the ghost chili.

From the excitement level in the cafeteria at dinner that night, no one would have guessed that the Seneca campers had initially been angry about hosting a campfire for Summer Center. A week of preparations and the realization that this was their last Saturday night of camp filled the room with energy and giddiness. Every conversation at every table was about what was coming that night, from the decorations to the music to the food.

Abbot couldn't stop talking about what was coming either. "Those nerds are going to be *hosed*! We just have to make sure they eat the right fondue. Then they'll cover their marshmallows with chocolate and end up eating fire!"

"Actually," Zack said, "I had to change the plan a little bit."

RJ glanced at him, and Abbot stared. "What do you mean? You're not wussing out, are you, Zack?"

"No way. But a better opportunity came up. We ended up making these desserts that look like cells from biology, you know, since Summer Center kids like that stuff. And since I figured they'll definitely eat the cells, I put the chili on that instead of the fondue."

"Oh," Abbot said. "So the fondue's totally safe?"

"Yep," Zack said. "The fondue's totally safe, and really good. It'll probably go fast, so I actually set aside a whole pot of chocolate just for us."

"Ni-i-ice," Abbot said, bumping Zack's fist. "I guess sharing a bunk with Betty Crocker does have its perks."

"Ha-ha," Zack said, rolling his eyes.

"Franklin's coming over," Abbot said. "Does he know about the change of plan?"

"Not yet," Zack said. His nerves taking over, he suddenly felt the need to stuff himself with food, even though his stomach was maxed from dinner and sampling fondue and cytoplasm all afternoon. He was downing his glass of lemonade when he saw Abbot sit up straighter, a sure sign that Franklin was there.

"Hey, man," Abbot said to Franklin.

"Hey," Franklin said. "Hey, Zack. We all set with the plan?"

"He changed it a little," Abbot answered. "They made some nerd food that looks like something from biology, so he put the pepper in that."

Franklin chuckled. "Yeah?"

Zack turned to look at Franklin. He was a big guy. He hoped the campfire wouldn't make him angry, because it was too late to change anything.

"But you used the chili?" Franklin asked.

"Yeah, I used it," Zack said. "It should be pretty funny."

"It'll be *hilarious*," Abbot said.

"It will be," Zack promised. "But you know"—he took a breath—"I was thinking. After this, after tonight? I think we should leave the nerds alone. Let's let them enjoy the last few days of camp in peace."

"I agree," RJ said.

Franklin looked at RJ like he was a mannequin that had suddenly come to life.

"I'm RJ," RJ said.

"Franklin." Franklin sized up RJ, considering. Then he cocked his head and patted Zack on the shoulder. "Sure, man," he said. "The pepper should end the summer on a high note. Why not go out being nice guys?"

"I was thinking the same thing," Abbot said quickly. "I'm going to be an angel after tonight."

Zack and RJ exchanged looks.

"But tonight is going to be classic," Abbot said. "Thanks to my idea."

"Yep," Zack said. "All thanks to you."

Chapter 42

GABE

As worried as the Summer Center campers had been about having to spend a Saturday night with Camp Seneca, as the sun set and the campfire neared, most of the anxiety was replaced by anticipation. Gabe and the Sssquad had done their best to spread word of the truce, but even those who hadn't heard were in good spirits; it was hard to be unhappy about a big party at night around a campfire, even if sworn enemies were going to be there too.

Without the pressure to dress for Nerd Pride, Gabe and his bunkmates just dressed their best. Gabe gelled his hair, Nikhil put a travel-size floss in his fanny pack, Wesley wore his favorite socks underneath his sandals, and Three O'Clock clipped on a tie. As they filed out of their cabin and joined the crowd on the way to the glowing party on the field, campers skipped and hugged and talked excitedly about the properties of fire, debated approaches for roasting marshmallows, and recited poetry about the moon. Gabe didn't feel the need to be the leader now; he was just proud to be part of this crowd.

"Wow," Wesley said as they got closer to the party. "I thought it'd be just a fire pit and some food."

"Me too," Nikhil said. "This is so much cooler."

And it was. A large square of the field was blocked off with tall posts. Each pole had a lit torch on top. White Christmas lights were strung between the posts with glowing paper lanterns descending every few feet. Two sides of the square were lined with tables, some filled with trays of hot food and others with cups of soda. The tablecloths that draped to the ground were lavishly decorated, the highlight being large, glittery letters that spelled out CAMP SENECA and SUMMER CENTER. Real, adult waiters in black pants and white shirts walked around with trays of graham crackers and marshmallows on sticks. Big pots of chocolate and cheese fondue sat over small, contained fires in every corner. And in the center of it all, surrounded by big stones, was the giant, smoking, sweet-smelling campfire.

"Wow," Wesley said again.

"Wow squared," said Gabe.

"Wow cubed," said Three O'Clock.

Amanda and Jenny came up to them holding empty plates. Amanda's hair was long and straight, like it had been on the first day of camp, except for one spot at the back that she must have missed with the blow dryer. Jenny's black hair was pulled back in an elaborate display of bobby pins, and she had a line of chocolate dripping down her chin.

"Have you tried the chocolate fondue?" Jenny asked. "It's so good." She went with Wesley, Nikhil, and Three O'Clock to get some.

Amanda stayed by Gabe. Gabe's palms got clammy. He fidgeted with the hem of his shirt. Should he compliment her outfit or something?

"I don't see the cytoplasm," Amanda said.

Gabe glanced around, happy to have something to do. He didn't see it either. He hoped Zack had actually made it. But even if he hadn't, the Senecas did seem to be fulfilling their end of the peace treaty. They were on the opposite side of the campfire, hanging out and laughing and leaving the Summer

Center side alone. If Gabe had had his map of the campground, he could draw a line down the center of the field, marking each side as an independent nation. Or maybe the whole field would just be neutral. Either way, it was all he could have asked for.

As he and Amanda stood there in silence, a group of three people dared cross the invisible boundary between the two sides. One of them was Zack. "Hey!" he said, grinning like crazy. "Do you guys like the fondue?"

"It's awesome," Amanda said.

"Isn't it?" said the guy next to Zack.

"This is my bunkmate RJ," Zack said. "And my friend Lauren. She helped cook too. Guys, this is my stepbrother, Gabe."

"Hi," Gabe said. "This is Amanda."

"Gabe's best friend," Amanda added, looping an arm through Gabe's.

Gabe gulped and kept his eyes on Zack. "Did you guys end up making the cytoplasm?" he asked.

"Yeah," Lauren said. "It's *so* good. They're saving it for later, after the skits and stuff, as a special treat."

"Okay," Gabe said.

"Are you guys busy?" Zack asked, glancing over his shoulder to the Seneca side of the party. "I want you to see something."

Chapter 43

ZACK

Zack noticed a lot of Seneca eyes looking his way as he led a group of Summer Center campers into Seneca territory. He kept his gaze straight ahead and his walk confident so as not to reveal the jitters running through him about what he was about to do. Franklin and his friends huddled nearby with some older girls. Abbot had just arrived and was talking to Leo and Maddie. Zack could sense Gabe's nervousness as they approached them. Zack knew he must have recognized Abbot from that first night when they'd gone into Gabe's bunk—he hoped he recognized him, at least.

"Just stay here a second," Zack said to Gabe and Amanda. "Hey, guys," he said, walking up to Abbot's group.

"I haven't tried the fondue yet," Maddie said with a flirtatious smile. "There's such a long line to get some, it must be amazing."

"And I don't see the *special* dessert," Abbot said, motioning with his chin toward Gabe. "I hear that's really, really good too," he said loudly.

"Yeah," Zack said. "They're saving that for later. Best for last. The fondue is great, though. I figured there'd be a line, so I hid a small cup just for us. Go get some marshmallows; I'll get the cup." He jogged away to the end of the tables and reached under the tablecloth, where he'd hidden a small cup of chocolate fondue, just the right size for dipping a single marshmallow. He brought it back to the group, his heart pounding. *Abbot would approve of this prank*, Zack reminded himself, *if it weren't aimed at him.*

"It's a *small* cup all right," Abbot said.

"Come on, man," Zack said. "This is all I could set aside. I was thinking of you."

Lauren gave him the same suspicious look she'd given earlier in the kitchen. Zack gulped, remembering her words. *Are you planning something mean?*

"It's the thought that counts," Maddie said. "I think that was very sweet, Zack." She laid her head on his shoulder.

Maddie would approve of this plan too, Zack thought. *Do I really want to do something Maddie would approve of?* He switched the cup of chocolate to his other hand, casually shrugging off Maddie's head.

Abbot took his stick and dunked the marshmallow into the cup. Some chocolate spilled over the sides, and Zack made sure to not let any of it touch his fingers.

Zack saw Gabe watching expectantly, his eyes magnified behind his glasses. Zack would have deserved it if Gabe had chosen to sabotage the fondue. Gabe's friends would have approved too. But instead, Gabe had proposed a truce.

Abbot raised the chocolate-covered marshmallow. Zack had no doubt that Abbot deserved to take a bite.

Abbot opened his mouth wide.

"Wait!" Zack cried. "Don't eat it."

"What?" Abbot asked. "Why not?"

Zack smiled awkwardly. "Because there's ghost chili in the chocolate," he admitted. "I put that whole entire chili in this one cup."

"What?" Lauren, RJ, and Gabe shouted in unison.

"What?" Abbot asked. He extended his arm to hold the marshmallow as far from his mouth as possible.

"We called a truce with Summer Center," Zack told him. "I put the chili in this cup for you to eat. I thought it'd be funny."

"Oh. My. God." Maddie's jaw opened, her gum sitting on her tongue. "That would have been hilarious."

"You didn't make cell stuff?" Abbot asked Zack.

"We did," Zack said, "but it's totally safe. All the chili is in this one cup of chocolate. I don't think you should eat it."

Lauren held up her hands. "You shouldn't even touch it."

Franklin and his friends came over and patted Abbot on the back. A drop of lethal chocolate fell off the marshmallow, and everyone jumped back.

"What's up, guys?" Franklin said.

"Zack called a truce with Summer Center," Abbot said. "He didn't spike the cell stuff."

"What?" Franklin squawked. "Dude, I was looking forward to someone eating ghost chili. I thought this campfire would actually be fun."

Zack thought it'd be hard to let Franklin down, but he found himself totally unfazed. He *was* bummed, though, that no one was going to eat a ghost chili. He wanted to know what one million Scoville units would do. "I'll try it," he volunteered.

"What?" Lauren screeched.

277

"I'll just put a little bit on my tongue," Zack said.

"You're crazy," Maddie said with admiration.

"We can't let this ghost chili go to waste," Zack said. "Someone has to at least try it."

"Dude," said Franklin. "You're hardcore."

"I'll do it!" Abbot volunteered. "Who dares me to take a whole bite?"

"What?" Gabe said.

Without waiting for anyone to dare him, Abbot shoved the entire marshmallow into his mouth and pulled it off the stick. He froze the second it touched his tongue. His eyes got wide and his face turned white. He looked around in a state of panic. His eyes started to water. He tried to spit, but the sticky marshmallow and melted chocolate clung to his mouth. "Aaaaaaaahh!" he screamed, piercing the air and fanning the fire, the brown and white goop vibrating between his upper and lower teeth.

Every head, nerd and non, turned toward them.

"Wa-wa-wa," Abbot panted, swiping at his tongue with his hands.

"What do you want?" RJ said.

"Water?" Zack asked. He looked around, trying to find some.

Abbot ran away, fanning his face, knocking through the

huddle of Franklin and his friends and colliding with the drinks table. He grabbed a cup of soda and sloshed it into his mouth, then sprayed it out. He did the same with three more cups, each splash sloppier than the last.

By now, every single person from both camps was watching Abbot as he tried to extinguish the fire from his tongue.

Nikhil came running over and pulled a carton of milk and a piece of bread out of his fanny pack. "I saved these from dinner, just in case there were hot chilies here after all," he said.

Abbot grabbed both and pushed them into his mouth. After a few moments, he had quenched the heat enough to stand still and stop pouring soda all over his face. The counselors, the Seneca director, and the camp nurses surrounded him, checking to see what had happened and if he was all right, but Abbot walked away from them and back to Zack and his friends, his eyes leaking tears.

"Holy ghost chili," Franklin whispered.

"Are you okay?" Maddie asked.

Abbot shook his head. Zack held his breath.

The Seneca nurse came back over and said she was going to make sure he didn't need to go to the hospital.

"Dude," Abbot said before walking away with her. "That was awesome."

Chapter 44
GABE

The rest of the night went along as well as it could have. The sour-apple cytoplasm was a huge hit. Some Seneca campers did skits, though none were as entertaining as Abbot's ghost-chili performance. Gabe was glad Zack had breached the camp boundary, but he and Amanda went back to the Summer Center side as soon as they could. Gabe would have plenty of time to hang out with Zack during the year—this was the last Saturday of camp, and he wanted to spend it with his geeky friends.

"Well," Nikhil said toward the end of the night, "it doesn't seem like anyone is going to die tonight, not even that guy who ate the chili."

"And no one fell in love across enemy lines," Wesley added. "Phew."

"I don't know," Gabe said. He motioned with his head to the table with the few remaining edible cells. Three O'Clock was there, engaged in an animated conversation in Korean with a girl from Camp Seneca.

Nikhil gasped.

"Go, Three," said Wesley. "We do have a few days left."

The SCGE director stood on a chair in the fading light of the fire and bleeped a bullhorn until she had everyone's attention. "What a night!" she said. "Before we all head to the cabins, Summer Center, can we please give Camp Seneca a round of applause for hosting such a wonderful party?"

The SCGE side of the field clapped.

The Camp Seneca director got up on a chair next to the Summer Center director and broke out his own bullhorn. "Camp Seneca," he called, "let's give a round of applause to Summer Center for hosting us all summer!" The opposite side of the field clapped.

"We know that relations haven't always been smooth the past five weeks," the SCGE director said.

"But I am confident that this campfire will kick off a week

of friendly relations," said the Camp Seneca director, looking around at his campers and ordering with his eyes for it to be true.

"I think," said the SCGE director, "that this campfire should become an annual tradition."

"I agree," said the Camp Seneca director.

A nervous hush fell over the party.

"But next year," the Camp Seneca director continued, "we can host you, just for one night, on the new and improved, fully rebuilt . . . Camp Seneca campground!"

Both sides erupted in cheers as though their last battle was to see which side could make the most noise. Gabe caught Zack's eye across the fading fire and gave him a thumbs-up. Zack returned the gesture with a fist pump. Then Zack went back to celebrating the news with RJ and Lauren, and Gabe was engulfed in a group hug from the Sssquad. The celebration continued on both sides of the field. The two camps were united in happiness, and no one could have said who had won. This wasn't about winners and losers at all.

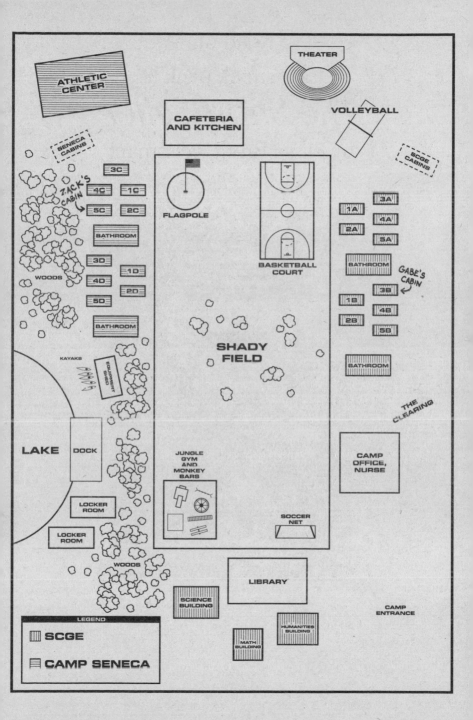

Read on

for a sneak peek at

The Short Seller

by Elissa Brent Weissman!

Lindy yawned and weighed the options on the table. She could start her homework, or she could start eating her plate of warm minicookies. Like there was even a choice. She stacked two of the cookies and bit into them together.

"Double-decker," Howe said. "You should eat one at a time so they last longer."

"Nah," said Lindy. She sucked a blob of melted chocolate off her finger. "That's no fun."

Howe slid into the booth opposite her and looked upside down at the books spread across the table. He barely even glanced at Lindy's plate of cookies, which didn't surprise Lindy but still amazed her. Somehow his dad being a baker had made Howe immune to the allure of sweets. Lindy thought if *her* dad worked at the Sweet Escape, she'd eat nothing but dessert.

"Are you ready for the math test on Friday?" Howe asked.

"Ugh, of course not." Lindy laid her head on her arm. "Steph's going to help me when she gets here. You should sit with us too. I can use all the help I can get."

Howe didn't try to hide his dislike for Steph. "I have to help my dad," he said, nodding toward the counter. "But if you have questions, you can call me later."

Lindy lifted her head, looked at her math book, and ate her third cookie. "Expect a call."

The door chimed as it opened, and Howe slid out of the booth, which meant it was Steph who'd entered. She was decked out in winter gear, including gloves, scarf, hat, and long, puffy coat. The hood of her coat was up too, creating a spaceman-effect with just her eyes and nose visible. Her family used to live in Arizona, where it was always warm, so they prepared for the New Jersey winter the way they would a trip to Antarctica. Lindy knew Steph didn't wear all the layers just for warmth, either. She had never owned a coat or any winter accessories before moving, so now, three years later, the novelty still hadn't worn off.

"Hey, Lindy!" Steph said as she began removing layers. "Hello, Howard."

"Hey," Howe said. He stuffed his hands into the sleeves

of his gray Windbreaker, his only jacket, no matter the weather. "I have to go help my dad. Later, Lind."

"Bye."

Steph slid into the booth, piled her clothes next to her, and shook out her long brown hair. "Why does he always leave when I arrive?"

"Maybe because you call him Howard. He hates that name."

Steph smiled. "That's why I call him it." She helped herself to one of Lindy's cookies. "I stopped next door and picked up the new *Teen Power*," she said. "It's got five pages of quizzes."

"Let me see," Lindy said. She and Steph were suckers for quizzes. They liked ones that promised to predict your future, but even better were ones that claimed to interpret the present. "'Are You Too Stressed?'" Lindy read. "If the answer is yes, do you think my mom will let me stop doing chores?"

"Probably not. Parents never appreciate the truth of magazine quiz results."

"'What's the Best Hat for Your Face's Shape?'"

"Ooh," said Steph. "What do they suggest for a heart-shaped face? That's what I have."

Lindy looked at her friend and realized that her face

was kind of shaped like a heart, with her center-parted hair forming the perfect bumps at the top.

"What shape is my face?" she asked Steph.

Steph didn't even need to consider. "Oval."

"And Howe's?" Lindy asked.

"Circle."

Lindy looked at him behind the counter and saw that Steph was right. His face was round, while her own was longer. Clearly, Steph had given this some thought before. "Impressive," she said. She went back to the magazine. "'Who's Your Celebrity Twin?' I hope those answers are better than 'What Is Your Spirit Animal?'"

"Shh!" Steph said, grabbing the magazine back from Lindy. "We promised to never speak of our spirit animals."

It was true; the results were too humiliating. Steph's was a sperm whale, which was embarrassing on multiple levels, and Lindy's was a bull, which Lindy thought was exactly that.

"Here we go," Steph said. "'Are You Really Best Friends?'"

"We know the answer to that," said Lindy. "How about 'Will You Be Able to Do a Triple Axel Next Week?'" she said. She and Steph were starting ice-skating lessons next week, and they'd taken to trying triple Axels in their living rooms, in the hallway at school, and even as they walked down the street.

"We know the answer to that!" Steph said. "We're going to be naturals."

"Okay, then," said Lindy. "Do they have 'Are You Going to Pass the Math Test on Friday?'" She frowned. "I think I know the answer to that, too."

Steph sighed and put the magazine away. "All right," she said. "Let's work on the homework."

But the minute Steph started talking through the first problem, Lindy began to lose focus. Something about numbers just made her zone out. She tried to concentrate, but she found herself wishing she could lie down right there in the booth and fall asleep.

"Hey."

Lindy blinked. Howe was standing at the side of the table, and he was holding a paper plate full of chocolate-chip cookies that were a deep brown.

"Do you want these?" he asked. "This whole tray got kind of burnt, and my dad was going to throw them away, but he said you could have them if you want."

"We don't need your cast-off cookies, Howard," said Steph.

"I wasn't offering you," Howe said. "I was offering Lindy."

Lindy looked at the cookies. "Thanks," she said, "but that's okay."

Steph smiled sweetly, but Howe just stared at Lindy. "Are you okay, Lind?"

"Yeah," she said, "I'm just really tired for some reason."

"Too tired for free cookies?" Howe said.

"No one wants your burnt cookies, Howard," said Steph.

Lindy rubbed her eyes. She wasn't in the mood to listen to them argue, and she certainly wasn't in the mood to focus on homework. "I think I'm going to go home. I'll call you guys later."

Steph pouted. "You're just going to leave me here?" she said.

"Leave you here, in the Sweet Escape, surrounded by deliciousness?" Lindy laughed as she filled her backpack. "I think you'll survive."

On her way out, she held the door open for Cassie, another girl from their class, and they smiled at each other.

"Hey, Cassie," Lindy heard Howe say. "Do you want these cookies? They're a little burnt, but you can have them for free."

"Serious?" said Cassie. "Awesome!"

When Lindy tackled the math again after dinner, she was too tired to even be frustrated. She stared at the page until her eyes started to blur. Then she blinked, and the words and numbers came back into focus. But it didn't matter; they made as little sense in focus as they did blurry. She just wanted to go to sleep.

Her sister, Tracy, squeezed past on her way to get a Twizzler. "You're *still* working on that?" she asked.

Lindy lowered her head on to her paper. "I'm just no good at math." She lifted her head and slumped back into her chair, her forehead smudged with ink.

"You're not good at keeping pen off your head either," Tracy said. She rubbed Lindy's forehead with her hand as she passed again, and Lindy didn't even bother knocking it away.

"You're not bad at math," her mother said from the kitchen.

"I'm not *good* at it," Lindy said. "I wish everyone would stop telling me I am."

"They tell you because you are. You're even in the advanced class. Math just doesn't come quite as easily to you as everything else does, Melinda, so you have to try a little harder with it."

Lindy laid her cheek on her homework, not caring about adding more ink to her face. It was just taken for granted that she was good at math because she was good at all the other subjects. Last year when she did too poorly on the test to qualify for advanced math in seventh grade, her parents and teachers had decided that it must have been a fluke since her other scores were so high, and she was put into the advanced class, anyway. "It doesn't matter how hard I try," Lindy said to the crease of her book. "Math just doesn't make any sense to me." She rotated on to her chin and looked at her mother. "Can I go to bed? I'm really, really tired, and my throat kind of hurts."

"Maybe that's because you spent forty-five minutes on the phone with Steph, even after you hung out with her at the Sweet Escape," said Tracy.

"Whatever," Lindy murmured. "Like you *never* talk on the phone."

"Um, no, I don't," said Tracy. "Talking is so junior high. I text."

"Girls," said their mother.

Tracy shrugged, stuck her Twizzler between her teeth so she could use both thumbs to type on her cell phone, and walked down the hall to her room.

Mrs. Sachs wrinkled her forehead with a mixture of concern and suspicion. "You do look a little out of it. But it's only eight thirty," she said. "Keep at it for fifteen minutes. I bet you can knock out the whole page."

Only if I were good at math, Lindy thought. She sighed and reread the third problem.

Her dad came into the kitchen and searched the pantry. "I saw Tracy with a Twizzler," he said.

Tracy, whose bedroom door was mysteriously soundproof when she was being called for dinner or asked to help with chores, reacted immediately. "You can have *one*, Dad! I had to clean the bathroom *twice* to make Mom buy Twizzlers."

"A clean bathroom and Twizzlers in the house," he said with a wink at Lindy. "Win-win for us."

Lindy gave him a half smile and looked back at problem number three.

Mr. Sachs downed his Twizzler in two bites. Then he

picked up the phone, dialed a number, and shook his head. "Jim's not picking up his phone. I need to get the name of that stock I was telling you about"—he waited another few seconds before hanging up—"but he's not picking up."

"So? Talk to him tomorrow at work."

"That could be too late. The sooner we buy, the more money we'll make."

"So ask him first thing in the morning, and then buy it at work."

"I can't. The trading website is blocked at work, so I can't place the order until tomorrow night when I get home, and by then the stock market will be closed, and so we won't buy until Wednesday morning, and by then the price might have doubled."

Lindy looked up from her page of math problems. "What are you guys talking about?"

"Nothing," said her mother.

"Stock," said her father. "This guy at work was telling me about a company whose stock is really low but going up quickly. I wanted to buy some, but I don't remember the name, and he's not picking up his phone."

"What do you mean 'buy stock'?"

"Don't worry about it," said her mom. "Focus on your math."

"When you buy stock, you buy shares in a company," her dad explained. "They cost a certain price per share, and you can buy as many shares as you want. Then if the price of the stock goes up, you can sell your shares, and you make money."

"So the price changes?" Lindy asked.

"Right, it changes all the time. Jim told me shares of this particular company have a low price right now, so that's why I want to buy before it goes up."

Lindy wrinkled her ink-covered forehead. "Could the price go down?" she asked.

"It could," said her father. "There's always that risk when you buy stock."

Lindy thought. "So if it goes down, would you lose money?"

"If you sell it after it goes down, yes," he said. "Say you buy one share for five dollars, and then the price goes down to four dollars, and you sell your one share—"

"You'll lose a dollar," Lindy finished.

Lindy's mother patted her on the back. "And you said you're not good at math."

Lindy's shoulders sank. Why did she have to be reminded about math? "It's been fifteen minutes," she said. "I can't stay awake anymore. I'll finish this in homeroom tomorrow."

"Lindy . . ." But her mother sighed when she saw the dark half circles under Lindy's eyes. "All right, sweetie. Get a good night's sleep."

"Thank you." Pulling herself up from the table felt like pulling a towel out of a bucket of water. She leaned over to kiss her mother good night and almost lost her balance.

"Whoa, Lindy," her mom said. "You really don't feel well, do you? Let me feel your forehead."

"I'm fine," Lindy said, leaning away. "I just need to go to sleep." She said good night to her dad, who was trying unsuccessfully to reach Jim again, walked into her room, and fell onto her bed. *I should change into my pajamas,* she thought. But her next thought was that she had to remember to give a box of burnt cookies to her Hebrew school teacher or else her grandfather would fine her four dollars. The part of Lindy's brain that was still awake told her that she should at least get under the covers before she began to have weird dreams about burnt cookies and Hebrew school, but the other part said, *Who cares?*

And so her parents found her an hour later: lights on, jeans on, on top of the covers, fast asleep.

Something strange is happening at Mumpley Middle School. . . .

by FOWLER DeWITT

illustrated by RODOLFO MONTALVO